MYSTERY AT THE ALASKA FISH SITE

DONNIS STARK THOMPSON

Illustrated by Jack Gaughan

Buff, a sturdy Alaskan youth of sixteen, will initiate his younger cousin, Todd, into the intricacies of salmon fishing. Their fishing site is an arm of the sea, with volcanic mountains in the distance.

Accustomed to big city comforts, Todd at first finds the relentless, continuing hard work almost more than he can take. There are huge, heavy nets to stake out in the water—and the tide, which rises quickly, can become a steep, dangerous wall of water. The boys eat, sleep, and work by the tide schedule.

Buff keeps saying that Alaskan fishermen are the friendliest people in the world—but Todd has his doubts, and then his suspicions—about Vimri, their nearest neighbor.

The action gets really rough when Buff and Todd discover that their first king salmon have been stolen. Pursued in the dark night, they must flee from rising waters as well as deadly bullets, before the villains are caught and a clever gun-smuggling scheme is revealed.

MYSTERY AT THE ALASKA FISH SITE

Mystery at the Alaska Fish Site

* * *

by **DONNIS THOMPSON**

Illustrated by Jack Gaughan

CRITERION BOOKS
NEW YORK

Another book by this author
THE LOON LAKE MYSTERY

CONTENTS

MYSTERY AT THE ALASKA FISH SITE

I THE MYSTERIOUS NEIGHBOR

It was May in Alaska and the jeep slithered through the breakup mud and on down the steep hill. Todd grabbed the iron rim that had once held the windshield of the battered old vehicle, a veteran of an Alaskan homestead beach site. It sported no top, no doors, and just about no motor. He glanced down at the canyon that fell away from the road on either side.

"Buff!" he shouted to his sixteen-year-old cousin, "Do you think it's safe?" His teeth clicked together and chattred. He wasn't sure whether it was from fear or cold.

Buff turned to him and grinned, his blond hair blowing in the wind. "Heck, no!" he said cheerfully. "Say! if you're cold, just turn on the heater."

Without thinking, Todd looked down at the rusted, raggle-taggle dashboard to follow the suggestion. Then he heard Buff's roar of laughter and he grinned back sheepishly. But he *was* cold! Just this time yesterday he had been in Chicago, telling his mother and father and brother Jamey goodbye. It was a nice, warm spring day in Chicago with gay jonquils blooming in the green lawns they passed on the way to the airport. He had gotten out of school a few weeks early and told his less fortunate classmates goodbye. (He didn't know whether he'd ever recover from all the cramming he'd done to take his exams early). The rest of his family was leaving too, accompanying his mother and father on a business trip; but he had elected to return to Alaska where he had spent the previous summer with Buff and his parents. Imagine, jonquils! Why here, back in the woods, he could see big banks of snow. The leaves were just barely budding on the birch, cottonwood, and aspen and, except for the evergreens, the woods looked gray.

Just then with a terrific bouncing and bucking the jeep hurtled over deep ruts and onto the beach, at the end of the twisting road. The seat shot into the air, Buff and Todd both bouncing higher than the windshield frame. But the bumping was forgotten as there, before them, was the most beautiful view that Todd had ever seen.

"Ohmigosh," he said, awed. "Ohmigosh. I've seen miles

and miles of pretty lights from our apartment window and I've seen hills and trees and I even thought your homestead at Loon Lake was something—but wow!"

The jeep came to a near stop and Todd gazed out over the waters of Cook Inlet, which was a huge arm of the Pacific Ocean. Twenty or thirty miles or so across the Inlet lay a range of snow-topped mountains. The tallest peak had a cleft in the top, or a "hole in its head" as Buff put it. He told Todd it was named Mt. Redoubt.

"Isn't that mountain something? Then that next highest peak you see there is Mt. Illiamna."

"I still can't believe it. The only thing I've ever seen that could begin to compare with it is a calendar picture of Mt. Fujiyama in Japan."

Buff put the jeep into four-wheel drive as the tires settled into the sand and they drove down the beach. The cold salt air coming off the Inlet made their eyes water. Buff kept up the geography lesson as they drove parallel to the waterline. "See just below Mt. Redoubt—in that kind of indentation—that's a glacier. You can see several of them. Oh, look, Mt. Illiamna's smoking."

Todd looked quickly and sharply at the thin tendril of white-looking smoke coming out. "Do you think it will erupt? Are there live volcanoes around here?"

"Which do you want answered first? Yes, there are live volcanoes here, but I don't think we need worry. They shoot off smoke every once in a while. There was quite an eruption a few years ago; covered Anchorage with ashes. Hey! Look! Neighbors!"

Buff wheeled the jeep to a stop as he came alongside another vehicle that showed similar signs of wear and tear.

"I wouldn't exactly say that Alaska fishermen and homesteaders put on the dog when it comes to cars. I'll bet they never heard of status symbols."

Buff grinned at Todd. "No, but they've heard of mud and salt water. Let's meet this guy. You'll never find friendlier people in the world than the beach fishermen. If we're going to live on the beach this summer and fish, we want to know everyone all up and down the line."

Just as the boys got out to approach the car, the man inside revved up the engine as if to leave.

"Hi, there," Buff called. "My name's Sanderson. Do you fish here? We'll probably be neighbors this summer. We're fishing the old Tolson fish site." He had to extend his hand clear inside the car before the man rather slowly and, rather reluctantly, shook it. In the open, Alaskan manner, Buff went on, "What did you say your name was?"

"I didn't," the man said shortly. Then he added, "Vimri. Pete Vimri."

"Oh, then, we *will* be neighbors. Your site's just on down the beach from ours, isn't it? Well, Mr. Vimri, I'm certainly glad to know you. This is my cousin, Todd. He's fishing with me this summer. He's from Chicago. My dad will be here with us off and on. He's working on our homestead. It's out north." There was a pause and a silence.

Buff smiled broadly, and tried again. "Well, we'll probably see a lot of you this summer."

14

"I keep to myself," the man said dourly, "and I like others to do the same." With that, he let the clutch out with a jerk. Buff's hand fell away from the side door.

Together, Buff and Todd stood there in the sand, watching the vehicle disappear up the beach.

"Well, I'm sure glad to get to know these friendly fisherman up here in Alaska. Why, you know, back in Chicago if you'd stop someone like that, he'd hardly give you the time of day."

Buff reached over and roughly tousled Todd's hair. "Gee, it's good to have you back. I'd forgotten how crazy you are. But, you know, this time you've got a point. I don't know what to make of that. That's the first time anything like that has ever happened to me. What did I do wrong?" His big, blond countenance that usually held a smile and a sunny look was now in a troubled frown. "I don't understand it."

"Well, if you don't understand it, I don't like it."

"What do you mean?"

"I mean we've gotten into a peck of trouble before when we ran into things you didn't understand."

But Buff didn't smile at this "remembrance." He kicked aimlessly at a mound of sand. "Oh well, who knows? Let's go. We've got several miles of beach to drive yet before we get to our site and we don't want to get caught by the tide."

The two boys raced back to the jeep and jumped in. "This not having any doors sure saves time, doesn't it?" Todd yelled.

"Nothin' like it," Buff answered and, as the jeep bounced

over the sand, he continued, "and not having any top saves getting your head bumped."

"Most considerate."

As they drove on, Buff pointed out the various fish sites that he recognized. "Here's Wilson's—an old man and his two grandsons live there—that place right next is Kesner's. That's a married couple that fish it—lots of women help fish." There were tiny shacks built at the bottom of the cliffs, some with names from last season still painted on them.

"The way this works is that the state licenses the fishermen and the gear. These beach sites have to be 600 feet from the next net and each person is allowed or licensed as many as three sites. They really check them, too—walk them off with a tape measure sometimes. So, this site of Walton's goes from here," he pointed out the glassless window, "about up to that waterfall that comes down the cliff. He can set three nets along the beach here. But, besides that, if he wants, he can set them way out in the Inlet—just as long as they are 600 feet from the next net."

"It's very confusing to me, but maybe I'll learn. By the way, I hate to be first-gradish, but how do you set a net?"

"That's what we're going to find out real soon; but, in general, we set stakes way out on the flats at low tide and put a pulley in and run a rope, a real heavy line, through it and up to two other stakes far up on the beach. The whole thing makes a triangle. We call it a running line. Then on one side of the triangle, where both ends of the rope meet, we tie the net in when it's time to fish. When the net is tied in, we pull the running line—that pulls the net into the water. When the fish period is over, we have to get the net back in, take it out, and then just tie the two ends of the running line together."

"That sounds so simple, I doubt if I understood a word you said."

"You're smarter than I thought. I worked down here almost one summer, just pulling on ropes it seemed. It was weeks before I figured out what in the world we were doing. It isn't simple—or, maybe it is. I'll ask you next August and see what you say then."

"What does the net look like? I mean, how does it catch fish?"

"Well, let's see. It's just a net. One side has floats that make it stay up in the water (the top, you might say), one side has a lead line that makes it sink. Oh, I know—it looks sort of like a tennis net with one end way out in the water and the other, up on the beach. At high tide both ends are under water. The fish try to swim through it as they go up the Inlet to spawn in the streams and lakes, and they get caught. If they try to back up, their gills catch in the mesh. In fact the fishing here is called *gillnetting*."

"I think I see."

"Good. I'll give you a test right after supper."

Todd groaned. "Don't mention the word test to me. I've taken so many lately, I eat 'em, dream 'em, and even brush my teeth with them."

17

Buff smiled. "Gee, it's good to see you again. It was a long cold winter; sometimes I thought it would never end. But now you're back and it's summer."

Todd clutched his coat about him. "*It is?*"

"It is, Kiddo, and if you don't believe it, just stick around some time until January." With that, he wheeled the jeep up near the cliff. He had been driving close to the water's edge because, as he told Todd, the washing of the tide made the surface there harder and more smoothly packed than the soft sand. The jeep settled down and almost stopped. Buff put it into super low. "Oh, oh. This is getting soft up here. But with these high tides coming, it will pack down again pretty soon."

The jeep ground to a stop and Buff turned off the key. They were in front of a weather-beaten shack, built right next to the cliff, and standing up on piling.

"Well, we're home."

Todd stared about him. The cliff rose sharply behind the cabin. In front of it the sloshing surf, rising now, foamed and pounded just 50 yards away from the shack. Beyond the water, soared the majestic mountains. The boys were all alone.

"You know, Todd," Buff had pulled a small yellow book from his pocket, "we just made it at that. That old tide is really coming in." The book, as Todd was to learn, was a tide book and life was to be lived by it.

"What do you mean, we just made it?"

"Just that. At high tide today, we couldn't have driven the beach. We're stranded. Didn't I tell you?"

"I'm not sure. I don't remember." Todd looked again at the water. "How high does it get?"

"Well, it depends. The tides change. We're starting in on the big tides right now. That's why we had to get down here. The tide comes in real high, but it also goes out real low and, when it does, we can walk out on the flats and set our stakes. Now, tonight, we're going to have a, let's see—" he studied the book, "a 20.1 foot tide." He showed the book to Todd and ran his finger down the long rows of figures. "Look, I'll show you. This is for Seldovia so we would add about an hour and a half to it to get the time of the high tide here on the beach where we are. So, at five thirty tonight, the tide will be 20.1 feet high."

"My gosh. Does it really work?"

"You can stake your life on it and—you may have to. You had better learn to read this tide book. Just about everything depends on it."

Todd was to realize later how true this was. He would eat, sleep, work by the tide. He would drive to town or not drive to town; drive to the neighbors or not drive to the neighbors according to the tide. He would learn he could never put down a bucket, tie up a boat, lay down a jacket without figuring where the tide would be and how it would affect things an hour or a half day from then.

Buff was frowning. "You know, since the earthquake, this beach has settled several feet. Some people say it is still settling and no one is quite sure where the safe places are any more; I mean, what height the tide will reach. I suppose we had better find some piling or boards or something and see how far up this cliff we can run the jeep."

"What do you mean?"

"I mean to get out of this tide. It will be high tide in a couple of hours."

"You mean the water comes clear to the edge of the cliff?"

"On the real high tides it does. If there's any wind, that pushes the water even higher. These aren't the highest tides yet. We get them 22 feet or so."

The significance of these figures was beginning to dawn on Todd. "You mean the water actually rises 20 feet? That's as high as a building."

"That's right—and it's all spread out on this beach— covers up about 200 feet from low tide. Just think of a 20 foot wall of water coming in. That's what it amounts to. I suppose, just to be safe, we'd better get the jeep up. As I say, the tide didn't always come so high on this beach, but the whole country dropped in the earthquake." He put the tide book back in his pocket and got out. "Let's size the situation up, take care of the jeep, and then get ready for the night."

They got out, walked up and down the beach looking for a likely place to pull the jeep up the cliff. Finally, Buff found a spot where a small spring had cut into the grassy bank, making a mound that looked almost negotiable. Together, they pulled up pieces of driftwood to build a sort of ramp. "Look at this, Todd, just look!"

"I see it, but so what?" It looked like an ordinary telephone pole to him.

"It's great. It's a great big piling that's washed up. All sorts of things get torn out and washed away and deposited somewhere else. Tomorrow, if it's still here after tonight's tide, we'll try to pull it up with the jeep. We need all the posts and pilings we can get—use them to reinforce under the cabin, or to tie running lines to, or to build driveways for the jeep, or to set the fish box on up out of the way—"

Todd looked anew at the big brown post. "I'll be darned. To me, it just looked like something in the way. I'm just not used to thinking about such things."

"You will be. You will be."

They heaved and pulled and worked at the ramp. "Now, let's try. You give me directions and I'll nose the jeep up the hill. Maybe it's not necessary, but I'm afraid not to until I know more about this beach. Just a few feet will help." Buff started the jeep, checked to see that it was in both four wheel drive and super low. "Okay, are the wheels going to hit the ramp?"

"I guess a little to the right. No, that's making the front wheel spin out. No, back up." But the jeep wouldn't back up. It was high centered.

"Gosh, Buff, I guess I told you wrong. I'm sorry. I don't know much about such things."

"Oh, don't be sorry. This sort of thing will probably go on all summer. We'll just have to get it out."

Todd looked about. "How far would we go to get a wrecker?"

21

Buff looked at him, disbelieving. "A wrecker? You don't go get a wrecker. You just get yourself out."

"Oh. I guess so. Tell me what to do."

"We're not stuck so bad. We'll just do a bit of shoveling and try it again. I think if we put another plank right here—" he pointed at the right front tire. Then he looked behind him. "The only thing is, we might be running low on time. Look at that water!"

Todd turned and looked about. "Ohmigosh. It sort of came up on us, didn't it?" There were the dark waves inching ominously close, like a noisy monster; coming slowly but surely onward. Where they had struggled with a heavy piece of driftwood just thirty minutes ago, there was now nothing but ocean.

Buff looked grim. "Let's get this jeep out. What if I've figured wrong? Who knows how high this darned water will come?"

Frantically, he dug out under the front wheel. He tried to lift with a log, using it for a lever. He pushed brush and logs under. "Let's try it again, Todd. Now, here's where I *want* this wheel to go." Even though it was still cold and windy, there were beads of perspiration on his forehead.

He jumped in the jeep and pushed on the starter. There was a sick, little hum. "Oh, NO." He jumped out, dashed in front of the jeep and threw up the rusted hood. He made some mysterious bumps and bangs and then called. "Todd, get in and try it now."

With a feeling of panic, Todd jumped in the jeep, bumping his knee on the way. "Let's see now, I just turn on the key and push down on the starter?"

Buff was nodding his head. "Keep your foot on the clutch. It may be in gear, then push down hard with your foot on the starter."

With pounding heart, Todd did as he was told. But no matter how hard he pushed on the starter, all he got too was a little hum. Buff called to him to stop, to try it again, to hold it, to try it without pushing on the accelerator, to try it with the accelerator all the way in. Todd decided not to look over to his right where the water was growing and growing.

Buff leaned against the jeep. "Well, if it isn't going to start, do you suppose we could jack it up somehow?"

"I don't know, Buff. I guess we couldn't put a rope around it and around that tree and pull it up any ourselves —no, I guess we couldn't budge it. What will happen if the water does get into it?"

"Salt water wouldn't do it any good. If it got clear into the engine, it would probably wreck it completely. It wouldn't be the first one around here that the tide had gotten . . . let's try it one more time. Ready? Go."

This time, there was a tiny sputter. "Keep it up! Keep it up! There. Keep pumping the gas, keep pumping it." The jeep was running, a bit rocky and uneven in its sounds, but running.

Buff banged down the hood and came around. "Don't let it die. I think I know the trouble. I'll work on it tonight, but now, let's just get it up the side of this hill." Ever so cautiously, Todd edged away, leaving his foot pumping the accelerator until Buff was in control. Then he jumped out.

24

"Okay, Buff, easy now, a little more to the right."
With great straining and heaving, the Jeep began to climb.
It came out of the hole. Buff gunned the engine and sent
it scrambling and bucking four or five feet up their ramp.

"Todd! Put some blocks under the wheels. We'll leave
her here." The jeep seemed almost straight up and down.

Together, they surveyed their completed project.
"There," Todd said. "I hope we can leave it there for
the summer. That's one thing done."

"For the summer? It comes down after high tide in a
few hours if it will start. We'll use it all the time in
fishing."

"After high tide? You mean all that work for just a
few hours?"

"That's the story of fishing. Hey! Look, we're about
out of house and home." The tide had risen to the piling
on which the cabin stood and the bottom step to the
porch was under water. "I can wade the water with
my rubber boots, but how about you?" He glanced at
Todd's leather shoes. "Better not. I've got some boots
packed away for you but we'll have to get in the cabin to
get them. I'll tell you, we'll put down another ramp and
go in from the back." Buff started up the hill, then called,
"Going my way?"

Glancing behind him, Todd said, "I can't say I have
much choice."

Buff found a 2 by 12 plank on the hill left over from
last year's fishing. "Just the thing." He laid it from the
porch of the cabin to the hill. "There's your bridge across
the moat. Be my guest."

II THE NEIGHBOR GETS A STRANGE VISITOR

When Todd struggled awake the next morning, he had a hard time remembering where on earth he was. The cot was hard, the one-room cabin nearly bare. He heard the sound of a motor outside so he pulled himself up to the small window ("porthole" Buff had called it) and looked out. It may have been only a peephole, but the view was vast: beach, ocean, and mountains. He took his eyes from the wonders of nature and concentrated on a woebegone pile of rusted tin: the vehicle was laboring down the beach and a small figure seemed to be headed away from it and toward the cabin. As the person came nearer, Todd could make out that it was Buff— but such a dejected looking specimen!

Todd hopped out of bed, pulled on his trousers and shirt, and went out on the back porch. The cabin built high on piling afforded a sweeping view up and down the beach. He watched the vehicle pull in at the next fishing site below theirs, then he waved.

Buff waved back, as he continued toward the cabin and up the steps. "Hi, Todd."

"Hi, yourself. I sure was a sleepy-head. I'm sorry. You're going to have to learn to roll me out. I'm not much of a fisherman yet." He glanced at Buff's frowning face. "What's the matter, Buff?"

"I wish I knew. I don't know what to make of that guy, Vimri. I just hailed him as he drove by. He had a load of stuff on the back of the pickup with a tarp over it and I barely touched the flap of the tarp and asked him if his nets were in good shape. Why everyone does that and we all load our gear up like that and—"

"Well, what about it?"

"He grabbed it out of my hands and told me to mind my own business. Doggone it, Todd, maybe I shouldn't have, but it was just neighborly. I didn't mean anything. We do it all the time—"

Todd could tell that Buff was feeling both guilty and frustrated, as if he had been scolded for doing something he shouldn't have—but didn't quite know what was wrong

27

about it. "Well, don't blame yourself and don't feel bad. If what you did was normal, then the fault must have been his."

Buff looked puzzled. "Fault? He didn't do anything wrong. I guess I did. I just don't know why he's so touchy."

"There you have it. What did he have in the back of the truck?"

"I don't know. I didn't look. But I suppose nets. Why?"

"I suppose it wasn't. If he didn't want you to look in the back, there must be something there he didn't want you to see. Maybe he's a spy."

For the first time, Buff's face crinkled into a smile, then he laughed. "Vimri? A spy? Boy, they must be hard up for spies these days." He reached over and roughed up Todd's hair. "You've been seeing too many movies. But then you always were a crazy kid. Naw, he's just a funny guy. Like you say about those people in Chicago: just not friendly. I guess I've been too forward with him. I've got to learn how to handle him."

"I'm from Chicago so I guess Vimri and I should get along just fine—if you think everyone from Chicago is like that."

Buff started for the door. "Okay, you handle Vimri. He doesn't like me anyway, I guess, and I'll handle breakfast."

Inside the cabin, Buff started getting out bacon, milk, eggs, and other cooking staples. They had been so tired last night, they hadn't unpacked much.

"Want to make yourself useful, Todd? Grab a bucket

and go out and pick up some coal on the beach. We've got to start a fire to cook with."

"Pick up coal?"

"Sure. It just washes up on the beach. You know what it looks like, don't you?"

"Oh, sure. Some of my farm cousins burn it all the time. I'm a real expert on coal," he frowned, "only I thought it was dug out of the ground."

Buff grinned. "Well, out on the farm, I don't imagine it was washed up on the beach."

"You got a point there." Todd took the pail and walked out into the sand. The sun was up, but he thought ruefully, it wasn't much help. He buttoned his coat tighter and set out looking for coal. All sorts of things had drifted onto the beach. There were shells, pieces of driftwood, pretty rocks, a feather or two, and a waterlogged boot. It was hard to concentrate on his search for coal. The waters of the Inlet pounded below him, much farther away now than when they came last night. He walked down to get a closer look. He climbed a rock and looked across at the mountains. He filled his pockets with pretty shells. Then he found a real trophy: part of a small octopus. He grabbed it up and raced toward the cabin.

He held it out for Buff to see. "Well, all I can say, Todd, is that it has seen better days."

"Yes, but isn't it great? Isn't he a little fellow?"

"Sure is. How's the coal coming?"

"The what?" He struck himself on the forehead. "Oh, Buff, I'll get right at it. I forgot."

29

"Where did you leave the bucket?"

"Right down by the water's edge. See?" He pointed out the window.

"Okay, but I want to warn you: right now the tide is going out so it's okay; but if the tide were coming in, you could sure lose things that way."

"Gosh, I'm sorry, Buff. I never thought."

"I know. That's why I'm telling you. Until you have been where there are twenty and thirty foot tides, you just can't believe it. But, say, we'll have to hurry and eat so we can get out there. The tide's going out fast and when it's at the lowest, we want to set our stakes out. Want me to help you with the coal?"

"No. I'll do it. Truly I will. Besides, I'm getting hungry."

Todd dashed out, ran down the beach, and grabbed up the bucket. However, the soft sand was harder to run on than he thought and he found himself panting from just that little exertion. He looked near the cliff and, sure enough, there were pieces of coal. "Not very good quality," he said aloud, pretending to know, "looks like slate—bet it doesn't burn very well." Gingerly he picked up a piece, remembering how dirty coal was; but as he dropped it from his hand, he noticed how clean his fingers still were. Curiously, he rubbed a piece. Slick as a whistle. "Well, I'll be darned," he told the world about him, "clean coal!"

He was so busy picking up coal that he scarcely noticed the vehicle that was approaching, until it stopped near him, and the driver leaned out. "Hey, Sonny."

Todd looked up. The truck was a shiny new yellow

panel truck. The driver looked as if he might be Japanese. "Yes, sir?"

"Can you tell me where Vimri's site is?"

Todd tried to act the way Buff did. He walked over to the truck and stuck out his hand. "My name's Todd Sanderson. Buff Sanderson's cousin. I'm going to fish this site with him."

Abruptly and hurriedly, the man extended a hand and shook hands briefly. "Yamasaki. Now, where's the site?"

Todd's face shone with enthusiasm. "Yamasaki?" Without considering whether he were being polite, he went on excitedly, "Gee, Mister, are you Japanese?"

The man hesitated. "You might say that. There are a lot of us here and there's lots of interest in Japan in Alaska fishing. Now, where's the site?"

"Is that right? You know, I just got here. It's hard for me to realize how close we are to Japan. You know, I was just thinking that when I looked at Mt. Redoubt, the only prettier thing I ever saw was Mt. Fuji—"

"The *site*?"

"Oh, yes, Vimri's is the next one down the beach, at least that's where his truck pulls into. But have you ever seen Mt. Fuji—"

But Mr. Yamasaki had already let out the clutch and the truck lurched forward. Todd's hand fell away from the side of the door. He stood looking at the vehicle for a moment, a frown on his face. Then he picked up the coal bucket, filled it, and walked thoughtfully to the cabin.

"Hi, Todd. Thanks for the coal. Now we can get some

31

food going. Who was that you were talking to? I wanted to come out because we really should get to know all our neighbors, but I was too busy just then." He indicated a bowl of pancake mix.

Todd handed over the bucket of coal. "Oh, another Chicago fisherman."

"What are you talking about? Who was it?"

"A Japanese named Yamasaki. He wanted to know how to get to Vimri's place and he was just about as friendly as Vimri. Didn't you say that was like people from Chicago?"

"All right, you win. I didn't mean *Chicago* exactly, just any big city. Maybe people there are friendlier than I thought, and maybe Alaskan fishermen aren't as friendly as I said. But I don't get it. *What is the matter with us?*" Buff dexterously laid the fire, and lighted it while he talked. Then he got a frying pan out and started the hot-cakes.

"You can wonder all you want what's the matter with us. I don't think anything's the matter with us. I think it's with them. I even started to talk about Mt. Fujiyama and he didn't act as if he'd ever heard of it—or cared. What kind of a Japanese is he anyway? Aren't they proud of their mountains? Why, if I was in Japan and someone said something to me about the Grand Canyon, why I'd—"

"Okay, okay," laughed Buff. "He's rotten at being a Japanese. Maybe he's never even been to Japan. Maybe he's never even heard of Mt. Fujiyama. After all, there are a lot of Japanese living in Alaska, especially in Anchorage."

"No, I don't think so because he said, let's see, he said something about there being lots of interest in Japan about Alaska fishing."

Buff turned a pancake, then looked at Todd. "Really? Did he say that?"

"Yes," Todd said, pleased that Buff found it important. "He really said that. Why?"

"Oh, because he's right. There's been a lot in the papers about the Japanese fishing in Alaska waters, and about the Japanese market for our fish. . . . I wonder. . . . You didn't ask him if he was buying fish, did you?"

Todd looked dumbfounded. "Why, *no.* Should I have? I didn't know people bought fish that way. Don't you sell them to large canneries or something? Who are we selling to? I never thought about it." He did so want to do things right. If only he could please this big, independent Alaskan cousin of his. "It's just that never in all my life have I said to a person, 'Are you buying fish?'"

Buff's voice was reassuring. "Sure, I know. It just would have seemed natural to me to ask. Yes, to answer your question, we sell our fish mostly to large canneries, although this year we're selling to a rather small operator. But, you see, the cannery operators send trucks along the beach to pick up the fish, and before the season gets started representatives from the canneries drive the beaches to get us lined up to sell to them. And, sometimes during the season, buyers will get desperate and go out looking for fish to buy. Some people are lined up with one cannery—owe them money or something—and can't sell to anyone else; but other people will sell to anyone. Sometimes the smaller operators will pay a few cents more than the big canneries."

"That doesn't sound reasonable. If the small ones pay more, why doesn't everyone sell to them? You'd think the big ones would pay more."

"It doesn't work that way. The thing is, the little ones *have* to pay more in order to get anyone to sell to them. As I said, most fishermen are lined up with the big companies because the big ones give lots of services: they loan money, have mechanics and boat repairmen around, serve meals and sell groceries, maybe give the fellows a place to stow their gear or put boats in drydock. When you're lined up with them, you sort of have a big brother behind you to lean on. The little canneries don't offer that. You hand them a fish, they hand you the money and that's it."

"I see. Very interesting. I'm really learning a lot." Todd was profoundly impressed. Back in Chicago, the kids he knew would be talking about records, or sports, or school. But here Buff was talking about the world of business like a grown man. "And I could do it, too," Todd thought, "if I had the chance. I'm not just a kid like Mom and Dad think."

"Yes, and you're going to learn more. And one thing you're going to learn right now: time and tide wait for no man. I guess you've heard that? Well, it's true. Boy, but it's true. Let's get around these pancakes and get out there. The tide is just about low right now."

As they bolted their breakfast, Todd noted with relief

that the hotcakes weren't the sourdough ones he'd had last year. "See you still use canned butter."

"Um-hum. Come on. Let's go. Don't clear the table. We'll get it later."

They bolted out the door and began a standard summer practice: run because the tide says you must; don't run because the tide says you mustn't; eat, sleep, get dressed because the tide demands it. Todd was still pulling on boots and jackets as he ran: Buff's sense of urgency was beginning to get through to him.

As they ran toward the receding water, they found themselves beyond the sand and on a huge mud-and-sand flat. Here and there they sank far down in their hip boots. Some spots were quite hard. There were shelves of coal and shale. Walking over one of these, Todd excitedly called to Buff. "Look at this thing I've found! What is it?"

"It's a sea anemone. You'll find them all along those coal and rock edges. In different colors too. We'll spend some time exploring up and down whenever we have a minute. Right now, I've got to get this stake in."

Todd had been paying hardly any attention to Buff. "My gosh, let me help you carry that." Buff was laboring along the flats, his hands and pockets full of supplies, dragging a sledge hammer. Todd gave him a hand and they went on until Buff saw a spot that suited him, very near the water's edge.

"Here, this is where we'll put the stake. Remember I told you we would put a pulley way out here and run the ropes through it, then bring our nets in and out by pulling on the ropes, or the running lines as we call them."

"Yes, I remember, but I guess I didn't really understand what it was all about."

Buff began pounding on the stake with the sledge. After about four strikes he was gasping for breath. "Boy, oh boy, that's hard work."

"Here, let a Chicago kid do that for you." Eagerly Todd grabbed for the hammer. It didn't even budge. He glanced at Buff, then pulled with all his might. Puffing and panting, he raised the sledge, an inch at a time, over his waist level, then dropped it, hoping against hope that it would hit the stake. It didn't. Again he hoisted it up, groaning and grunting. This time it made contact and the stake gratifyingly sank a bit. Again he struck the stake, and again. Then he dropped the sledge and smiled at Buff. "This is hard to believe, but I feel shaky. How much does that thing weigh?"

Buff grabbed it up. "Oh, I really don't know. We use it for football practice up here in Alaska."

"I know, I know. I can just see a sixty-yard pass with that thing. I can't even get it up high enough to throw."

Taking turns, the boys finally had the stake just right, and the pulley secured to suit Buff. "Now, then, let's go set the others."

In weak, shaken tones, Todd said, "The others? I could have sworn this would be like the Taj Mahal—the only one of its kind in the world." But he obediently followed Buff down the beach. When the rising tide forced them to quit work on the stakes, Buff thought of other chores. There were ropes to be tied, ropes to be pulled on, ropes

37

to be spliced, and ropes to be wound into huge coils. Heavy, heavy ropes. Todd didn't understand *why* he was doing what he did. But if Buff said, "Pull," Todd pulled.

It was almost noon when the boys dragged themselves back to the cabin. Todd's mind was a haze of work projects: all of them heavy. "You know," he groaned, "it all comes back to me now from my last summer up here on the homestead: news about labor-saving devices not having reached Alaska yet." He threw himself on a cot.

Buff grinned, poured two glasses of milk, handed one to Todd; then seated himself at the table where he could look out on the beach. "Oh, I don't know. Think how hard it would have been to pound those stakes with a rock. You had a nice, shiny sledge to use."

After drinking the milk, Buff sighed. "Well, I think I'd better clear this breakfast stuff, get us something to eat, and then we'll take a rest. You're tired so I'll cook. You're a lousy chef anyway if I remember right."

Todd made a good-humored face at him. "If you really want to treat me, I think I'll let you fix lunch while I take a short walk along the beach."

"Are you kidding? I thought you were beat."

"I am, but I'm also curious, and I want to look at things when I'm not trying to push a jeep up a hill, hammer with a sledge, or run ahead of the tide."

"Right you are. Beaches can be fun, you know." He was secretly very pleased that Todd was so interested.

Todd slowly and unsteadily got to his feet. "Beaches fun? I have heard that, but I can't imagine where." He gave Buff a big grin and went out. He didn't want to tell

Buff, but he wanted to do some special exploring while Buff was occupied. He wanted to see what Vimri had in the back of his jeep. Besides, he was so tired already that he knew he'd never be rested again. There was no use even trying.

III TODD INVESTIGATES

Todd pretended to walk aimlessly for a moment just in case Buff was looking out of the window; then he headed toward the huge cliffs that rose abruptly from the beach. The cliffs were forested and he reasoned that he could sneak up to the Vimri fish shack more easily if he stayed close to brush. However, distances and sizes and shapes were deceiving on the beach. It was a great deal farther to Vimri's cabin than he had supposed. From a distance it was hard to tell whether there was anyone on the beach or whether what he saw was a rock, a piling, a log, a person, or something else entirely. However, Todd saw nothing that moved. As he drew near, he climbed along the slope to remain completely out of sight. From there he could look directly onto the Vimri location. Like all fish sites, the buildings and equipment huddled near the bluff to be safe from the tides. There was an extra shack or two here. Buff's location had only the cabin. Todd sat down and decided just to watch for a while. He could see Vimri's old vehicle and a bit of the bright yellow truck of Yamasaki's. So the Japanese was evidently still here, and evidently in the shack with Vimri. Todd slid carefully down the hill a few feet further. He could see Vimri's truck easily, the one Buff had tried to look into, before he was bawled out.

"There's nothing in it," Todd said softly. "Not one thing." Feeling like a trained detective and a knowledgeable fisherman, Todd looked about for the nets. "If Buff saw a load of nets, they must be around somewhere."

He slid down the hill further. He was now directly behind the cabin and in line with a back window. Cautiously, he looked about. No nets in sight, but he did notice that the two extra shacks sported big, shiny padlocks. Suddenly he heard voices and a scraping of feet or furniture. He paused. Did he dare? Slowly, he eased himself up from his sitting position and ever so carefully peeked in a corner of the tiny window. Vimri and Yamasaki were edging toward the door.

"Okay, I'll be shoving off. Guess the tide will let me make it out. Now, remember, the first load on the 9th," he said. "That would be, let's see, Wednesday. I'd guess at, oh, eleven o'clock. Be sure—" Whatever it was that Yamasaki wanted Vimri to be sure of was lost to Todd for the men were then outside the door. Todd could hear no more. He decided he had better scamper back up the hill keeping under cover of the brush, before he was seen by either or both of them.

Panting and grasping for roots Todd pulled himself up the steep cliff. Above the roar of the surf he heard the low drone of the yellow truck as it labored along the sandy beach. When he felt safely out of sight Todd struck off toward Buff's cabin, by way of the beach. Tired, perspiring, and scratched up from his encounters with sticks, brush, branches, and the thorny devil's club, he dragged himself inside.

Buff looked up from one of the cots. "Where in the world have you been? I hate to sound like a parent, but I kept wondering whether you were okay. I didn't see anything wrong out near the water so I just ate lunch and relaxed."

"Ate lunch? Already? Sorry. I took a walk up the cliff."

"I figured as much, but when you had been gone almost an hour, I thought you might be lost. Yelled a couple of times, but didn't get an answer."

"An hour? Holy mackerel! I thought I had only been gone ten minutes or so. I'm sorry, Buff."

"Well, okay, this time." He grinned sheepishly. "As I say, I've never been on the parents' end of an argument before. Come on, what will you have to eat? There's canned stew or canned stew."

"In that case, I'll have stew."

42

Buff took a pan from the stove and spooned some stew into a dish for Todd. They sat down at the table and Buff ate some crackers and peanut butter to keep Todd company.

"You, uh, you run into any devil's club or anything up the hill?"

"Yep. Ran into that and something else. I just happened to find myself right above Vimri's site and—" Todd tried to talk as he ate. "And while I was there, I thought I'd take a look in the back of his truck to see what was in it."

"Oh, no, Todd. You didn't! Look, we've got to be neighbors with that guy all summer. He's been mad enough at me. I guess he just doesn't want anyone fooling around his stuff."

"I guess not. Anyway, the vehicle is empty. There's nothing in it."

Buff shrugged. "So he dumped his nets off. Probably on the rack."

"The nets aren't anywhere unless they are right in front of the front door. I could see everywhere else for I was right behind his cabin and near his other little shacks."

"He probably has them in one of the shacks then."

"He must have something valuable in them."

"Why, what do you mean?"

"Well, all the doors have brand new padlocks on them and they are locked. The windows are boarded up. Can't see a thing. Is that normal?"

"No-o-o. In the winter or if he were going off for a time he might lock things up, but there's no sense in doing it when you're around all the time. Why, the Alaska fishermen are the—"

"Yeh, yeh, I know. The friendliest people in the world."

"Doggone it. Usually they are. I don't know what's going on up there."

"I've got a clue."

"What do you mean?"

"You know that Japanese I talked to this morning? Yamasaki? Anyway, he was there and they were talking and he told Vimri to be ready for the first shipment on the ninth, about eleven o'clock. He said that would be Wednesday. So, I guess you're right. I guess Vimri's just a nut and doesn't like us, and that Yamasaki is buying fish from him." Todd reached for another cracker, then paused, his hand in the air. Buff was staring at him in an exceedingly strange manner. "What's the matter, Buff?"

"Wednesday? Wednesday? Why, the fishing season doesn't even start for a couple of weeks. Are you sure you heard right?"

"Of course I'm sure. He said the ninth and then he said that would be Wednesday at about eleven o'clock. Does the ninth fall on a Wednesday?"

Buff reached into a drawer beneath the table where a calendar, a tide book, some papers and a pencil were kept. Hurriedly he consulted the calendar. "Yep. Wednesday is sure the ninth. It's only day after tomorrow. Todd, do you realize what this means?"

"No, except that Tuesday must be the eighth."

"It means that Vimri is going to start fishing before the

44

season opens. He's going to be fishing illegally and Yama-saki is going to be buying them illegally."

"I guess that's serious?"

"Sure, it's serious; but, mostly, it's just darned foolish. Why on earth would they take such a chance? Yamasaki can't need fish so badly that they'd take a chance like that to gain two weeks. They're sure to get caught."

Todd shrugged. "Well, I guess it's up to them. They're old enough to know better."

Buff sounded furious. "Well, they sure as heck are. I still can't believe it. Tell you what, we'll just keep our eyes peeled. We can certainly tell if they're fishing. You can see nets in the water even farther away than your nearest neighbor."

"Oh, good. We'll be the spies." Todd looked eager and delighted.

Buff had a hard time to keep from smiling. "Just remember what I said. We can see them from here."

They finished eating, and took short rests. Buff assigned Todd the job of dishes and housecleaning while he went out to begin checking on the nets.

"There's a broom, well, a broom of sorts. Just stack things on the shelves. Dad said the king gear needed repairing, so I'll go check that first. This is the first king season the Fish and Game people have allowed us for several years. We may not do too well but I want to try so we can get broken in for the red run."

Todd looked puzzled. "That part about the broom I followed. But what's a king? What's a red, and why does a red run?"

Buff smiled. "Ohmigosh, haven't we told you anything? I'm sorry. The king salmon are the huge salmon—the very best. You can't even buy them most places. Of course, I know some people sell king salmon but they just call it that 'Outside,' it's not our real kings."

"They're the best, huh?"

"Real delicacy. Real fat, lots of oil. We can them, smoke them. They're great. Best fish I've ever eaten. They don't even taste much like fish; I think they taste like real meat. In fact, you don't say, 'clean a king,' you say, 'butcher a king.'"

Todd was agog. "Really? How big are they?"

Buff's eyes were shining as he warmed up to his subject. "Sometimes you get a small one, and I don't know how big the biggest one is, but I've caught some myself that weighed over 50 pounds. I've heard of kings that weighed 100 pounds. Do you realize how big that is? It's as big as a person."

"Wow!" Todd stood leaning on his broom. "Why do you even bother with the others? Is that the main salmon?"

"No. There aren't enough kings. That's the trouble and why we haven't been allowed to fish for them much. The main salmon is the red salmon. Some people call them 'sockeyes.' We call it the *run* because that's when the big batch, or run, goes through the Inlet from the ocean back to the spawning grounds."

"Oh, yes, I've heard of that. We've had movies in school that showed salmon jumping over waterfalls and everything to get back."

"The one and the same! Right here in front of you."

Todd breathed out slowly and ecstatically, "Gee-ee. Kings and reds. I've got to remember that. Those are the kinds of salmon we'll catch."

Buff looked amused. "You'll remember that. By the end of summer, you'll know every kind just by looking at it. We get so much for kings, so much for reds, and I forgot to tell you, so much for humpys, and so much for silvers, and so much for dogs."

"Dogs?"

"Yep, dog salmon. Those are all kinds of salmon— humps, silvers, reds, kings, and dogs."

"Gee, I always thought the life of a fisherman was a simple one. I'll never even be able to remember all the names."

"Oh yes, you will. Well anyway, we get to fish for kings this year. It takes a certain size net, and we're supposed to have some king gear—nets, that is—on the back porch. I'll go take a look while you fix up the house."

"Roger." Todd began to sweep furiously, muttering, "Kings, reds, humps, silvers, dogs, kings, reds, humps, silvers, dogs—"

Buff stuck his head in the door grinning. "Oh yes, the kings are also called 'chinooks;' the reds, 'sockeyes;' the humps, 'pinks;' the silvers, 'cohos;' and the dogs, 'chums.'"

Todd's chant broke off into a groan and he stared at Buff helplessly. "If it's all right with you, I'll stay with the sweeping. A broom is a broom."

"I've heard them called 'idiot sticks'," Buff retorted as he walked out.

Todd picked up a small worn mat next to the door and there, underneath it, was a nice big crack in the floor. He got down on his hands and knees and peered through. There was nothing at all to see except beach some ten feet below. "Well," he marvelled. "Isn't that handy?" He started sweeping the dirt and sand down the crack. "I never was very good at taking dirt up with a dustpan. How simple to have a hole in the floor."

Feeling very satisfied with himself and his labors, he stood the broom up against the wall, looked about the clean room, sighed, and sank down on the wooden bench beside the table. Resting, he gazed out of the window and thought, Buff is right, this is really dining with a view.

"Alaska, Alaska," he began. "Boy, they really have mountains up here. Why didn't Yamasaki want to talk about Mt. Fuji? Adults sure are funny. Well, if he is going to buy fish illegally as Buff says, maybe he's got a lot on his mind to worry him." Todd hardly realized he was thinking out loud. He reached into the table drawer as he had seen Buff do earlier and pulled out a lined writing tablet and a pencil.

He wrote a letter:

> Shores of Cook Inlet, Alaska
> May Something (I'm confused)
>
> Dear Mom and Dad:
> I got here okay and Buff and I are staying alone at the fish shack. We nearly got the jeep covered with water last night when the tide

came in. We have strange neighbors who, we believe, are going to fish illegally. One is a Japanese. They seem tough but Buff says we will catch them at it. I swept the floor.

Your Son,
Todd

The more he read the letter, the better he liked it. He was sure it would reassure them and at the same time let them know how grown-up the boys in Alaska are. Maybe they would pay more attention to him when he got home and not treat him as such a kid.

He put the pencil and paper down. Gosh, but it was quiet! The tide was receding and the surf made a regular, peaceful sound. He listened intently, but he could not hear another thing. Then a tiny breeze pushed a branch against the shingled roof and Todd followed every scratching sound. "It sure is quiet here," he said aloud, and his voice rocketed into the room almost eerily. "What *is* it that makes so much noise back home? I can hear myself breathe here. I can even hear my heart beat." He looked about. How very strange everything seemed. He got up awkwardly, went over to the cot and flopped down. His muscles ached from the unaccustomed hard work. He wondered briefly where Buff was and what he was doing. Then he "heard" the stillness again.

Lying on his back, he stared up at the rough ceiling with its hanging cobwebs, the limp strings running from old nail to old nail, with a couple of rusted hooks for

49

lanterns. Buff had told him that the fish shack had been there since 1915. He wondered idly who had put those nails in. What hands had touched them? Had the hands belonged to a Russian, an Indian, an Aleut, or one of the wandering Scandinavians: a Norwegian, a Swede? For he knew, from talking to Buff, that various nationalities had been drawn to this beach for the fishing. He said, almost in a whisper, "If there are such things as ghosts or spirits or possibly spacemen trying to get in touch with us, I'll bet people living in this silence will be the first to know."

He had no idea how long he had slept or what time it was; but the sound of Buff clumping around woke him up.

"Hi! Are you awake? I'll bet you're starved. You looked· so tired I let you sleep through supper, but I saved some sandwich makings."

Todd gazed at him in a stupor. "Supper? Gee, I didn't mean to fall sleep. I'm sorry, Buff." He started up, then groaned. "Oh, am I stiff! I can't move."

Buff laughed. "Too hard on you the first day? For one thing, Todd, you were probably worn out when you got here—hurrying to get ready, catching planes, changing time zones, and all." He looked at the cot where Todd was struggling to get up. "Why don't you just stay there?"

Todd gritted his teeth. "I don't see why I should let sledge hammers and time zones get the best of me." He sank back. "On the other hand, if it's after supper, I don't see why I should get up." He grinned at Buff, then frowned. "If you've had supper, why are you putting on your waders?"

"Because it's almost low tide again and because we

didn't finish this morning and because I've got to get back out there."

"Great Scott!! You mean?" Todd pointed wildly in the direction of the water.

Buff laughed. "Is everyone from Chicago a clown?"

"That's right. Funny, but unfriendly." He dodged a boot Buff picked up and threw.

"All right, all right. So I goofed. So city dwellers aren't necessarily unfriendly. Say, you know, Todd. That reminds me of our neighbors again. I couldn't help wondering about them all afternoon when I was working on the nets. I sure don't see any sign of people hurrying around down there to get ready to fish. If they are going to pick up a load day after tomorrow, how are they going to have anything for them to pick up if they don't get busy?"

"Well, don't ask me. I wouldn't even know how to get a load of fish ready even if I could get out of bed."

"No, Todd, really. I'm kind of serious."

Hoisting himself to the edge of the cot, Todd groaned. "You think I'm not?" Then he added, "I know you're serious, Buff, but I haven't the faintest notion what it could possibly be. It's as if you suddenly landed in Chicago and heard people planning a big deal on buying and selling stocks or something. All I know is that they're weird characters and I don't trust them. As far as their fishing schemes and breaking rules and getting ready or not getting ready—you'll have to be the judge. Of course I guess you could go ask them if they're going to be ready in time to fish illegally."

He walked to the table, made himself a sandwich,

cocked his head on one side and said, "Is this some of Aunt Sally's canned moose?"

"Right you are! You're a real Alaskan to remember from a year ago what moose tastes like. Makes a pretty good sandwich, doesn't it?"

"Better than beef any day. Is this the moose you shot? The one you wrote about?"

"Yep. Right out on the homestead. It was really something. Moose had been scarce all season. Dad and Mom had both been hunting for days—walking, tramping all over, canoeing, driving back trails. Then, one Saturday, I took the gun and went across the lake in the canoe. It was a nice fall day, just a bit of light rain, enough to keep the bugs down. The leaves had turned yellow and were just beginning to fall. The cranberries were ripe and real heavy underfoot. Well, you know, just a perfect day: fall, no school, moose season. I pulled the canoe up along shore and tied it to a small birch that hung out over the water and, just then, I thought I heard a noise. I stopped to listen—hardly breathing. We really needed a moose and the season was going fast! Then I heard it again: a knocking. Sure as the world it was a moose banging its horns on a tree. They do that, you know. Well, I got out of that canoe and practically crawled up that hill, and when I had almost reached the top, I could see the moose. He had heard me and was standing still as a concrete post and looking in my direction. Boy, you just don't know how hard it is not to make *any* noise in the woods! Anyway, as I peeked up over the last rise and saw him there, I could tell he was getting jumpy and skitterish and ready to run. I looked just long enough to see that he had horns and to take aim. I didn't even stand straight up; shot from my knees. Hit him in the neck and he ran, oh, thirty yards before I got him again. He really crashed down. I ran up and put a finishing shot in his head. He was a beauty. You'll have to come back with me to the homestead to see his rack. Not the biggest rack of horns we've ever gotten, but the prettiest and the most even.

"Well, Dad and Mom heard the shots and knew what it was. They came over in the skiff and helped butcher it out. Took two trips in both the canoe and skiff to get him home. Gee, the folks were thrilled—but they felt kind of foolish, too. They had hunted so much." Buff grinned proudly.

Todd's eyes were shining and his hand holding the sandwich was shaking with excitement. "Wow!"

Buff smiled. "Well, anyway, that's what you're eating."

The only remark Todd could think of was "Wow!" so he said it again. Then he finished what he was eating and made himself another sandwich. "Tell me more about moose hunting, Buff."

"Sometime. Me and my big mouth. I've told you too much now. Great Scott, look at that tide! I've got to go."

They tore out of the house just as they had earlier in the day. As Todd grabbed jacket, cap, gloves and other pieces of wearing apparel, he said, "You know, this is getting to be a habit. Doesn't anyone here *ever* get all their clothes on before they run out the door?"

54

IV A HEAVENLY VISITOR

It was a chilly evening but fresh with salt-laden air and the cold-fresh smell of an Alaskan spring. The mountains over across the Inlet were still fat and pouchy with snow but the tops were tinged with the red rays of the evening sun. Todd had no idea how late it was. That much he remembered about Alaska from last year: worst place in the world to try to tell what time it was. It was seldom dark and the sun seemed to run around in crazy circles, with no proper comes-up-in-the-east-and-sets-in-the-west to it. He shrugged his shoulders. "Oh well," he

muttered, "as the Alaskans say, 'does it really *matter* what time it is?' It's just shovelling time, or planting time, or fishing time, or net-setting time."

They had been working almost an hour, pulling on cold, chilled ropes until their hands were red and almost numb, when they heard the drone of a motor. They looked up and down the beach and saw nothing, but the sound came closer and closer.

"Hey, Buff, look!" Todd excitedly pointed skyward. "It's a little plane and, wow! is he ever close, is he—Hey!" Todd crouched low as the small yellow plane roared down just above their heads. "My *gosh!*" Todd stared after the plane. "I thought he was coming down right on top of me."

Buff was laughing. "It looked as if you thought that. Say, he's landing down the beach."

"What for?"

"How do I know what for? Why do people drive cars or park them at certain spots? He might be coming for a picnic on the beach. He might be trying to see someone. It's not unusual. So many people up here have planes . . . H'mm. He seems to be landing right at Vimri's. I guess the sand is good there for landing. No, by golly, he's *going* to Vimri's. Look at that."

The yellow plane taxied close to Vimri's cabin. Suddenly there seemed to be a great deal of commotion. People were dashing back and forth between the cabin and the plane. Evidently there were two persons in the plane for Buff was sure he could count at least three running about, although it was hard to tell that far away.

Todd stood up. "What are they doing?"

"I'll be darned if I know. They must be unloading something. Yes, I guess so. Vimri must have sent for a load of stuff—groceries or fishing gear or something. You've heard of bush pilots?"

"You mean those fellows who operate a sort of private plane company— just fly people in and out of little places?"

"That might do for a definition. Anyway, bush pilots are famous in Alaska and there are lots of them. With such big areas and so few people and so many places with no roads or railroads, everything would just about come to a screeching halt without them. How else would people get to a fishing spot, a camp ground, an isolated mine, a homestead way back in—"

"Gee, that must be great. I think I'll be a bush pilot someday."

"No reason why not. You'd make a good one."

Todd felt a tingling glow at the words. Now that was like the things he had tried to tell his folks, and never succeeded. If a fellow said in a serious way that he wanted to do something, people should believe it. They shouldn't laugh and think of all the reasons why it wasn't possible. Just a thoughtful, "Well, go ahead . . . it might be okay."

Suddenly a roar rent the air. The yellow plane was already a few feet off the ground. It climbed sharply, banked, and flew back over the boys.

Buff was thoughtful. "Well, he sure was in a hurry, wasn't he? I never heard of a bush pilot yet who couldn't stay long enough to drink a cup of coffee, unless it was a real emergency."

"Oh, I don't know. I wouldn't stay long at Vimri's place

either. At least we haven't had too much luck being friendly with him."

Buff agreed. "Guess you're right." But the frown stayed. It surely was peculiar. The tide was going out so that could not be the reason for the hasty departure. The weather was good. Buff's frown was not lost on Todd. Apparently Buff thought it even stranger than he was admitting.

The boys went back to their tasks. It all became a blur to Todd who, by now, had put in a long day. "Hang onto this rope and pull it as tight as you can . . . Here, see if you can pound this stake a little more . . . Can you get this knot while I pull on the other end? . . . I need a bit of twine, could you run back and get me a piece? . . . Now, hand me the pulley . . ." It went on and on and, numb with fatigue, Todd tried to respond.

As the tide ebbed, then started back, the boys were driven up the beach, closer to the cabin. The shadows lengthened. Seagulls made a last half-hearted circle, careening above the boys' heads. Their calls sounded lonely and a bit sad. Lights flickered on in the cabins up and down the beach. Todd said, "Neighbors."

Buff answered, "Yes, but most of those lights are miles away. A light can be seen for a long, long distance."

For some reason, Todd shivered. Maybe he was just a little cold and very tired. But suddenly it all looked so big and so harsh. Just a few souls, really, in all this world of cold, mammoth tides; of towering snow-capped mountains, immense distances, and freezing, bone-weary-ing work. Would it ever seem friendly? He felt a little frightened. He thought bleakly, "Maybe my parents are right: maybe I'm just a little kid after all."

But at last Buff said, "Let's call it a day." Dragging the inevitable rope, and some tools, they made their way over the deep sand to the cabin.

Todd looked at the five steps leading up to the porch. "If there were only four," he told Buff wryly, "I believe I could have made it." But he half climbed, half crawled up them.

Buff rebuilt the fire quickly and soon the cabin was warmer and cheerier. He started some water heating for hot chocolate and opened a can of stew. Todd sank onto the bench and rested with his arms and head on the table. "I'm beat, Buff. I don't even care whether you fix supper. I'd just as soon go to bed."

"You'll feel better as soon as you eat. It won't take long. Then you'll sleep better."

But Todd didn't feel better. It wasn't just that he was tired, either. He couldn't shake the feeling of dread he had had on the beach. What had brought it on? Perhaps knowing he and Buff were so alone. Perhaps that plane at Vimri's. Even Buff had looked worried. It wasn't any one thing—just an atmosphere that suddenly seemed hostile and strange.

Buff reached in front of him and turned on the short wave radio. "Maybe this will take your mind off your troubles."

"Troubles? I guess my only trouble is trying to show my folks that I can work and earn some money so they'll know that I'm more than just a silly, irresponsible kid. I don't know, though. I don't think any of our parents believe us. I'm sick and tired of being 'too young'—not good for anything except to be told what to do, and what to believe."

"Hold it! Hold it. My parents let me act my age—and more. Sometimes I think life would be easier if they didn't. When they think of you as a grown-up, you have to behave that way, and sometimes it's hard. And I wish they had enough money to send me to college. I've *got* to go and they know I'm old enough to earn my way. So, here I am, not necessarily from choice. Maybe you're lucky and just don't know it." He grinned at Todd, trying to shake him out of his dark mood.

The squawks and the squeals on the radio settled down and the announcer said, "This is Radio Moscow."

Todd sat upright. "Radio Moscow?"

"Sure, we get it all the time. We're really not so far, you know. Most of the time it is broadcast in Russian; but this program is beamed in English to us—just as Radio Free Europe is beamed to them."

"Holy cow!"

Buff shrugged, but was glad Todd was thinking of something besides himself. "It's kind of fun. They say some wild things about our country—and theirs. But the music is good, whether it's this program in English or their regular broadcasts."

And so Todd sat that May evening, eating canned stew, drinking hot chocolate cooked on a stove that burned clean coal, gazing at the last dim outlines of the rugged, ragged mountains across Cook Inlet, and listened to a

Russian violinist. "Well, I'll be darned," he said, as it all got to him, "I'll be darned."

Todd awoke late in the morning with a tired, drained feeling. He got out of bed and went out on the porch in search of Buff. He found him mending nets.

"Hi, yourself. I thought I'd let you sleep. We don't have to be in much of a hurry right now. I'll work on nets a bit. Not much more we can do now."

Todd went down to where the nets were strung between two poles so· they could be spread out and mended.

"Nice day. I believe I could almost go without my long underwear and fur parka." Todd examined the nets.

Buff smiled. "You're just a sissy. You'll get used to it. Here—want me to show you how to mend nets?" He looked at Todd. "No, I forgot. You haven't even had breakfast, I'll bet. I'll show you later. Give you the morning off." He pointed in the opposite direction of Vimri's cabin. "I saw our neighbors on this side this morning. They seem to be gone again now. Name's Sundborg. Of course it is still plenty early to move in for the season, especially if they don't mean to fish for kings; but I don't know when they're going to get their outer stakes in if they don't hit these tides." He frowned.

"Well, they must know what they're doing," Todd ventured.

"I guess. It's just that everyone worries about everyone else."

"I noticed."

"Oh, all right. So Vimri doesn't fit." Just as he said that, the yellow panel truck came zipping down the beach, dodging rocks, sending sand aflying.

"Hey, it's that Japanese fellow I told you about—Yamasaki."

They watched as the truck roared by, several yards in front of them. The driver gave no indication that he had seen them.

"Well, he's sure in a hurry! He's a nut to drive the beach like that."

Todd began edging away. "You did say I could have the morning off, didn't you?"

"Yes, but, you'd better not—" It was too late. Todd was gone. Buff pondered a moment. He knew what Todd was up to. He was going to spy on Vimri again. Should he stop him? He really didn't like the idea very much, but, was there really any harm in it? Todd would just peer through the woods on the slope and see what was going on at the cabin; maybe catch a word or two, maybe not, depending on the wind. "Oh, well, it's just kid stuff," he said impatiently. "Besides, I'd like to know myself what in the world is going on there."

Todd climbed the hill directly behind their cabin and kept that distance up on the slope all the way to Vimri's site. It meant jumping a few gullies, going into some patches of thorny devil's club, and getting whacked a couple of times by brush and branches. Away from the water's direct breeze, mosquitoes buzzed, landed, and bit. "Oh, oh," he groaned. "I had forgotten about you fellows —you everlastingly miserable pests! But I remember now! I remember now!" At last, he arrived: scratched, bitten, and sweating. As he wiped his forehead, he marvelled that only a few minutes before he had felt so cold.

The yellow truck was in front of the cabin. Todd crept cautiously down the hill under cover of the brush. When he heard voices he stopped abruptly and knelt down. Apparently they weren't in the cabin. He decided he was safe for a few feet and inched down to where he could look around the side of the cabin. The men were standing near the truck and Vimri was talking.

Todd strained to hear the words but the man had his back to him. Then the voice rose. "When you say the ninth, you *make* it the ninth."

Yamasaki was getting into the truck. "Just take it easy. It all worked out. Now, remember, tomorrow. That's not a date so we're not going to get confused. Just—TOMORROW." With that, he started the truck, revved up the engine, wheeled about, and roared down the beach.

Todd turned quickly and crawled back up the hill. He was disappointed that he had heard so little of it, but he didn't want to stay any longer. Keeping out of sight and listening was one thing when the men were talking; but he knew how quiet it would be when Vimri was alone. He was afraid the man would hear or see him once Yamasaki was gone.

He worked his way back very slowly. He kept looking over his shoulder to see if Vimri was still out in front of the cabin. He didn't know why, but he felt uneasy, just as he had last night. When he was almost a third of the way home, he glanced back and gasped. Vimri was standing on the beach near his cabin and looking, it seemed to

Todd, directly at him. Todd automatically froze. His heart pounded. Was the man just shielding his eyes with his hands or was he holding binoculars? It was too far away to tell.

Then Vimri turned and disappeared from Todd's view. Sighing, Todd started again. When he was almost at the cabin, he came down the hill to the beach.

"Hi, Buff."

"Hi, yourself. How's the morning off—and the spying?"

Todd plopped down and rested his back on a piling that held one side of the net rack.

"Well, you're right, of course. I *was* spying and I got caught. At least, I think I did."

"Oh, no."

"Maybe, no; but I think, yes. At least he looked for a long time right where I was on the hill."

"Did he do anything? Try to hail you?"

"No. I was a long way from his cabin by then."

"Don't worry about it. If that's when he saw you, he probably didn't think a thing about it. After all, people go back and forth on the beach and up and down the hill all the time. Why should he think anything of it? Lots of kids climb hills."

Todd shook his head dubiously. "I don't know. I just know how I *feel*."

Buff laughed. "You feel guilty because you know you were spying. But Vimri doesn't know it."

"Let's hope you're right," Todd said fervently. "Something about that guy gives me the creeps."

"You haven't told me yet how the spying went. You

know, I don't think you had breakfast and it's almost lunch time. Come on in. You talk while I fix dinner. Did you get clear to the cabin?"

The boys went inside and Buff got some soup, and some peanut butter and crackers out for them.

"Well, I got to the place just as Yamasaki was leaving. All I heard was Vimri telling him something like, 'if you say the ninth, make it the ninth, and Yamasaki told him not to get so excited, that it all worked out okay."

"The ninth? That was when he told him to expect the first load of something, wasn't it?"

"Yeh. I guess so. The other day he said that. Oh yes, another thing: he said, 'Tomorrow.' "

"What do you mean, Tomorrow?"

"I don't know. But Yamasaki told him that there wouldn't be any mistake over dates this time because it was just *tomorrow*."

Buff chewed thoughtfully on a cracker. "In other words, whatever was to come on the ninth will come tomorrow, which is—the tenth."

"I suppose that's what he meant. No, No, it isn't. Because he said that it had all worked out okay. You know, like they had already had it."

"But they didn't fish yesterday. They didn't do anything —wait a minute! The *plane!* The plane came yesterday— on the eighth." Buff laughed. "We're a couple of goons. He just ordered some groceries or something and they were to come on the ninth and they came yesterday instead. Simple?"

Todd said tiredly and a bit grumpily, "Well, all I can

say is that they must have been very special groceries for all that fuss. You'd have thought Yamasaki would just have brought them in his truck."

Buff looked at him carefully and said slowly, "Yes, you certainly would think so. And why would he need more tomorrow?" He got up with a show of determination. "Tell you what. Let's load some rope and a piling or so and a sledge on the jeep and go up and work the running line nearest Vimri's. We just might happen to bump into him and, if we see him, we'll make a little conversation. After all, fishermen are—"

"—the friendliest people in the world," Todd finished for him.

The boys had only worked a half hour or so when Todd spotted their neighbor. "Hey, Buff, there he is." He pointed to the top of the shack. "What's he doing?"

Buff looked up at the fishing cabin. "Fixing the roof, I guess. Come on, let's go over."

"Do we walk?"

Buff hesitated. "Let's take the jeep."

"I'm with you. It has a better getaway."

"Goofball."

They hopped in the vehicle that was, for practical purposes, just an engine with a seat on top of it. They bounced over the short expanse of sand to the cabin. By the time they got there, Vimri was climbing down from the roof.

"Hi, there! How's it going?" Buff gave the man a big smile.

"Fine."

There was a slight pause.

"See you fixing your roof. Like us to give you a hand?"

"Nope, nope. I wasn't fixin' my roof, I was—well, yes, I was—but I don't need no help. I take care of my own affairs."

"Be glad to help if you run into any trouble. We're a bit younger than you and there are two of us." The man said nothing, but Buff continued, rather doggedly, "I see you had company last night."

Todd decided to help Buff out. "Yeh, that plane. Boy, that was something. He just came in and—"

"No. No, I didn't have a plane here."

Forgetting himself, Todd rushed on. "Oh, sure you did. We saw it. A *yellow* one. Why, I thought it was going to hit me. I even ducked down."

"Oh, yes. I had forgotten. Just some fella' wanted to find out where he was. Lookin' for some folks."

Todd's mouth fell open and he was about to go on, but suddenly Buff jammed the accelerator down on the jeep and the car jerked forward. "Well, so long, Mr. Vimri." They took off in an ear-splitting roar.

Todd grabbed the edge of the seat. "Talk about Yamasaki! You're a cousin menace."

"Sorry. I haven't hit a rock yet; well, I haven't hit a boulder anyway."

When they were a safe distance, Buff slowed down, then headed the jeep back to where they had been working. "Let's load up this stuff and go home." As they worked, Buff went on, "It's just that I didn't see any point in pushing him. He obviously didn't want us to know about the plane. But why?"

68

"Beats me. I don't understand a single thing that goes on in this country. Why should I understand why somebody named Vimri wants to pretend he didn't dash back and forth from a fishing shack to a bright yellow plane?" With many grunts and groans, Todd loaded the sledge in the pickup. "You know something else? I don't think he was fixing the roof. And don't ask me why a guy named Vimri climbs up to his roof, because I don't know that either."

Buff laughed. "You're a nut. But I kind of think you're right."

"Have you binoculars in the cabin, Buff?"

"You betcha'. And I'll tell you something else: from now on you're not the only spy. We're going to see what he's doing on his housetop and we're also going to see what will happen tomorrow."

"Tomorrow?"

"Yes. Remember? You said Yamasaki told him 'tomorrow.'"

"Oh, that's right. Tomorrow." The word seemed to bounce back and forth. The boys looked solemnly at each other. Then they drove back to the cabin.

V HURRIED PREPARATIONS

Buff dug out the binoculars for Todd. He put them on the window ledge. "Here they are. The next time we find Mr. Vimri up on his roof, we'll see what he is doing." He held up a cautious hand. "Now, I realize, we're probably being silly and there's probably a good, simple explanation for all that has happened, but—"

"—but you want to know what the explanation is," Todd ventured.

"Well, yes."

But the spying was put off for, just then, they heard the

sound of a motor and dashed to the door to look out. A man got out of a car and waved it on. "Why, it's Dad!" Buff dashed out the door.

The tall, thin homesteader who showed the signs of many seasons' weathering on his quiet, cheerful face, smiled and called, "Hi, boys."

The three went inside, all talking at once. Buff's father sat down and gazed about the cabin. "Not too bad for a couple of boys."

"I swept," Todd told him proudly.

"But what brings you down here, Dad? I didn't expect you for another week or so. Is anything wrong? Mom?"

"No, no. Everything's fine. I drove down to the top of the hill, started walking the beach, and got a ride. I came down to ask if you had been listening to the radio. They're opening up the king season for a couple of trial days. They didn't say, but it might be all the king season they'll allow. Sort of a test run to see how the catch and how the escapement goes. Thought you boys might just as well take a stab at it."

"When, though?"

"Monday."

"*Monday?*" Buff stared at him first incredulously, then in dismay. "We can never be ready in time."

"Oh, sure you can. I'll help this afternoon. They've been broadcasting it since yesterday but I just couldn't get down until now. Didn't you hear it?"

Todd said, "We listened to Radio Moscow and they didn't say a word about it."

His uncle grinned at him. "You're a couple of fine fishermen. Radio Moscow. Well—shall we get on with it? Let's go take a look. I can stay late because, by walking, I can go any time and not worry about the tides. At that, with these high tides, I'll probably have to climb up the hill here and there to keep my feet dry. I have to be back at work in the morning and I can't come here again before Monday. It's my only chance to help you boys so let's make the time count."

Then began one of the busiest afternoons and evenings of Todd's life. His uncle was saying, "All right, you have to have your lines ready, the nets mended, the buoys painted, a fish box made, and—how about the dory and skiff? Do they need patching? Let's just hope they don't need major repairs. Buff, did you bring the stuff down here to fix the boat? We'll have to pull it down, or maybe push it down with the jeep to get it in water."

As he tried to follow instructions and do the job allotted to him, Todd heard Buff say, desperately, "Dad, we'll never make it."

"Why, Buff, this isn't like you. Of course, you'll make it and, if you get only one net in the water, all right. Actually, it's so early in the season, I doubt that you'll get any kings. But it's experience and it's a chance for a few extra dollars. Besides, sometimes the very best way to get things done is in a limited amount of time."

When Mr. Sanderson left that evening, the boys were so tired, they were hardly functioning. Todd was trying to fasten ropes around the buoy kegs. These tied to the anchors out in the water made their "outer" locations a sort of tag of ownership and protection against any other claims. He suddenly realized he had been working at one little knot for a long, long time and he put the keg down.

"Buff," he said quietly. "I'm too tired. I'm not getting anywhere."

"I second it. Let's go in."

By mutual consent, they ate crackers and peanut butter again, and fell into bed. "One thing about Dad's coming. I know better now what has to be done and how to plan it . . . Oh, darn. I meant to listen to the radio tonight to see if there was any other fishing announcement, but I forgot."

But Todd did not answer. He was sound asleep.

The first thing in the morning, Buff sat down at the table and made a list of all the things he could think of that had to be done before nine o'clock Monday morning. He explained each one carefully to Todd. Then he rationed the chores for the four remaining days. "You might say this is our master plan. Any questions?"

Todd quickly scanned the list. "Yes. Where is something I can do? I don't see a thing on there about sweeping the floor or gathering coal."

"I consider you a full-fledged working partner. These are all things you can do. Such jobs as sweeping and cooking are extras that we each do when we have time."

Todd sighed. "I'm truly flattered. Besides that, I'm truly sore." He looked at his scratched, bruised hands. "I guess I'm supposed to start where I left off—with that knot on the buoy keg but, you know—" he worked his fingers. "My hand is so sore, I can't even close it."

Buff was sympathetic. "I know. That's why I put the buoy kegs on tomorrow's list. You should be more rested by then."

"Oh, really? What do I do this morning?"

"I thought maybe you could build the fishbox. We've got some scraps here and there—use any old boards you can find. We should put it high enough on the hill so the tides can't get it, but as near the beach as possible so we can load the fish into it quickly and be ready when the fish trucks come along."

"I don't get it."

"Well, when we pick the fish out of the nets—either on land when the tide is out, or from a boat when the tide is in—then we load them on the jeep and take them up to the fish box. It's just a storage place until the fish truck comes. The truck drivers stop at every fish site that they buy from, collect the fish and take them to the cannery. They have counters and give us a ticket each time which tells how many salmon of each kind there were in our load. Now, the box doesn't have to be tight—better if it isn't. Just so it will hold fish. We have to keep it shaded and, I think, we'll run a hose down from the spring and keep cold water running through it. Don't want to lose any from spoilage. Okay?"

"I guess so. How big do I make the box?"

"Oh, so big by so big." Buff made vague gestures that Todd interpreted to be about 6 feet by 6 feet. "It doesn't have to be enormous. They pick up on every tide so, unless we are just flooded with fish, there won't be any problem."

74

Todd armed himself with hammer and nails and went out to do a bit of salvaging and building. It sounded so simple, yet it was amazingly difficult. "Just crude carpentership is all he wants," Todd muttered as he struggled with boards that seemed to weigh six times more than they should. Starting the job, he at least began to see the problem. "Guess I'll need something underneath to nail the bottom *to*. Buff said we might have to pull it. Yes, it should have skids or some kind of a framework underneath." He was talking to himself as he puttered about.

"Buff! Buff! I can't find any kind of lumber that will do for skids or a framework under the bottom of the box. Shouldn't it have something like that?"

"Be a good idea for several reasons: the box will move easier and also be up off the sand. That way, the water we run through it will drain out. Keep the fish cleaner. Good thinking."

"I know," Todd continued, "but I can't find a thing that will do. We need something like a 2x4."

"Right, and a nice, slim spruce will be just the thing." Buff looked up from his boat-caulking job to add helpfully, "Woods are full of them."

With a sigh, Todd headed for the cabin to find an axe. It took a careful search to find a spruce just the right size; then it took chopping to fell the little thing and remove its branches. Nearly an hour later, scratched and tired, Todd pulled the spruce log up beside the box materials. He measured it off, sawed it, and was contemplating his work when Buff's shadow fell across the sand.

Buff smiled encouragingly. "That looks pretty good. Just about right."

"I think so too and I also think that I need at least two more just like it."

"Good thinking! Hey, you're catching on fast."

"Am I ever," he grumbled. But he picked up the axe and again climbed the bank to find his trees. At last three poles lay in place and Todd nailed the bottom boards for the box to them. Then he started on the sides. Buff had said it didn't have to be tight, just so it would hold fish. How big was a fish? How small a crack could they get through? He could find only a few more boards, none of them the same width or length.

"But I'm going to nail them up fast before he tells me that more spruce logs would be just the thing." He sawed off the boards to equal lengths, then discovered he had made a slight mistake. The sides couldn't all be exactly the same for there was nothing to hammer them to at the corners. He should have cut the ends an inch or so longer, so he could nail through them and into the other side boards. "Oh, gosh!" He was tired and hungry. "What do I do now? Let's see: what *can* I do?" He squinted his eyes at the box. "Well, if I had some 2x4's, I could make four corner poles and hammer the sides to them, but I don't have any 2x4's and I hate being a carpenter and I don't want to cut any more spruce logs, and I'm hungry."

He grabbed up the scraps of the spruce he had already cut. "Maybe a couple here might do." With reckless abandon he put the two into place and nailed the side boards to them. "So far, so good." He didn't even stop to put his next actions into words but by pounding and stretching, and pulling the box all out of shape, he managed to get the other sides nailed together. It was done! He stood back and surveyed the job. He ticked off the requirements, "Buff said it had to be so big by so big, and should be off the ground, and just tight enough to hold fish, and real sturdy . . . who said a box had to be square? I think a trapezoid is rather nice and salmon deserve something different once in a while."

He grabbed up his tools and headed for the house. "I'm done! I'm done!"

Buff had just finished eating. "Good for you. Come on in."

With that rare and expansive feeling of a job solidly accomplished, Todd sat down at the table and tackled his meal.

Buff was studying the master plan and Todd asked him between huge bites, "How are we doing?"

For an answer, Buff shoved the paper in front of him with a smile. "For your information, it's three o'clock."

"Three o'clock! Holy cow." He scanned the list quickly. "Let's see—well, I guess I'm about four hours behind already. Did it really take me that long? I started at eight and you thought I should be through at eleven and it's—holy cow!"

"I know. I'm not doing much better. Why is it that things always take longer than you expect? Here, want some peanut butter?"

"Yes, I guess so. Gee, I hope one of us gets finished early enough tonight to cook something."

Buff stood up. "I agree. So, I guess the only thing to do is to get going. Any questions?"

"Just one: why was it that I was so anxious to go to work and be an adult?"

Buff grinned and waved at him as he went out the door.

It was later that day when the tide was out that the yellow plane came over again. "Hey, Buff, Look." Todd shouted and pointed to the plane, but he couldn't make Buff hear. Forgetting how tired he was, he ran up to the next beach location where Buff was checking the pulleys on the running line. "Buff, look! It's the same plane."

Buff looked up and, together, the boys watched the plane land at Vimri's again; and, again, they could see a rush of activity.

"Remember? He said something about *tomorrow*. Buff, this must have been what they were talking about each time—that plane coming in."

"I guess so. Darn it! I wanted to watch them through the binoculars. I don't suppose I could get to the cabin in time; no, he's taking off already. Doggone it."

Buff watched carefully as the plane became airborne, rose in a graceful arc, and flew back over them. "Todd, that's the strangest thing I've ever seen. I was so busy thinking about our fishing, I forgot all about Vimri."

The boys finished their chores in thoughtful silence, then, as the tide forced them back, they quit for the evening and went to the cabin.

"Tired or not, I'm going to cook something," Buff said as he started the fire.

Todd groaned. "You're a better man than I am, but I'm glad you are. I can't move."

"Don't. After all, I've got some age on you—a whole year or so."

"That's right, so hurry up with that supper. Why, when I'm sixteen, I'll be able to work all day, cook supper, then go out for a game of football and not be the complainer you are." He ducked as a shoe sailed across the cabin. "Remember now, I'm just a little kid."

"I've noticed, except when it's time to come to the table and—it is."

With a rush, Todd dashed across the room and plopped down on a chair. "I'll have mine done medium-well."

"Medium-well done stew it is."

Todd groaned good-humoredly, "I hope they never stop making stew and peanut butter. You'd starve to death."

The boys sat and ate and gazed out the window at the red tips of the mountains.

"Hey, Buff! There's someone out in a boat."

Buff craned his neck for a better view. "Why, it's Vimri, I guess. He must be working with his buoys or his outer nets. Well, I guess he's going to fish after all. I'll bet we have lots of people on the beach tomorrow. Lots of them will want to throw a net in for this trial king season. It's a brand new idea. I don't think it's been tried before."

"Throw a net in. How easy you make it sound. Actually, it's the next thing to the Siberian salt mines."

Buff picked up the binoculars. "It's too dark to see very well, but I think that's Vimri, all right. He's really in a big dory. You could go to China in that. I wish I had had these glasses today when that plane came in. Oh, well. What difference does it make?"

"I hope none, but I don't know."

"What's the matter, Todd?"

"I don't know, but I feel creepy about the whole thing. I admit I don't know a thing about fishing, or the people, or their habits, but something's not right at Vimri's place. I just don't like the feeling I get."

"You're getting to be a spooky old woman, aren't you?"

But for once, Todd omitted his usual funny reply. The worried frown remained on his face as he said seriously, "Maybe, but I've got a strange feeling and I don't like it."

VI SPRING AND VIMRI COME

Buff was right about the fishermen showing up. On Friday, the beach was full of frenzied activity. "This may not equal downtown Chicago, but compared to the way it has been—Wow!" Todd exclaimed.

Vehicles piled high with belongings had gone by most of the day, the occupants waving gaily and grandly. One fellow stopped by to ask if they would sell him any kings they might get as he wanted to smoke them.

"Yes," Buff said. "I didn't know for sure what we would do with them since none of the canneries that I know of are open yet. Of course, no one *really* expects to get any kings."

The man smiled. "Well, you get the experience, some of us independents get a few fish for smoking, and the officials get some reports to study."

"I suppose that's about it."

As the tide came in, the traffic ceased and the boys were driven up near the cabin to work. Again they worked late and tumbled into bed. Usually, the high tide during the night awakened them: the surf was right under the shack and the waves sloshed against the piling the cabin sat on; but they were too tired that night to hear it.

As soon as Todd went outside Saturday morning, he sensed a difference: it was still, only a slight breeze ruffled the Inlet. The sun was shining, high and hot. There was not a cloud to be seen.

"You know, it's really going to get hot today," Buff said.

"I don't believe it. I don't believe it *can*."

"You have a short memory, but I agree. We don't have enough hot weather up here."

As the boys worked, the temperature soared. They began shedding jackets, and caps, finally shirts. All during the morning they talked about the weather. "Part of it is the lack of breeze, I guess. It's usually windy and kind of raw on the beach even in mid-summer."

Soon Todd called, "Buff, how hot do you suppose it is?"

"Must be near 70 or so. After it has been in the 40's and 50's that's quite a difference, you know."

"I know, I know."

By noon, the work slowed to a mere tap here, a pound there. Todd found himself staring into the distance, hypnotized by the heat. Soon he was stretched out on the sand. "I give up," he muttered.

Buff looked at him and hesitated. "Well—" but within seconds, he had joined him. "Just for a few minutes."

"This may be the only day the whole summer that it's like this: clear, hot, without a breeze. And, it's been such a long cold winter."

"Uh-huh."

"We'll have to make up for this, but we can do it when it gets cold again."

"Uh-huh."

"Let's face it: we probably won't catch any kings anyway. One net is probably plenty good enough to get in Monday."

"Uh-huh."

Todd felt as if he were made of hot, heavy sap. A fly buzzed about his face and he tried to shoo it away, but his arm was much too heavy to lift. He gave up.

A jet flew over, high, high above the Inlet. A few white gulls flew lazily about, then landed on a sand bar and sunned themselves.

"I'll bet the people that came to the beach today think this is really a great place."

"Uh-huh."

The boys napped and their faces began to turn beet red. Todd stirred. "You know what, Buff?"

Without opening his eyes Buff answered, "What?"

"It's the first time I've really been warm since I left the Chicago airport."

"Good."

"But, at that, my back's getting cold. The sand I'm lying on feels cool now. What did I do? Melt the ice underneath?"

Buff laughed and sat up. "No, but you are going to get your feet cold and wet in a minute. Look at that tide! Maybe we'd better go eat or something."

They scrambled to their feet and went into the dark, chilly cabin. "It just won't do. I'm not even in a mood for a fire to warm it up. Let's fix something and eat it outside."

"You're being very sensible, Todd. There's one thing you learn in the long, cold winters up here and that's not to waste a hot day, especially by working."

While they ate a sandwich on the porch Todd was staring at the hill behind the cabin. He couldn't put his finger on it, but something was decidedly different.

"Buff! Buff! Look at that hill! Look at those trees!" He jumped to his feet, ran down the steps, up the hill to the first little willow. He examined a branch. "Buff! The buds! I didn't see any this morning. They must be almost an inch long—almost leafed out. The hill! It's *green*!"

Buff followed slowly. "By golly, you're right. I've seen spring come fast, but never this fast."

"No one will ever believe me, but those buds have sprouted almost an inch in just hours."

The boys looked hungrily at the hill. Where there had been only grayness, there was now greenness; where

85

there had been only barrenness, now there was growth.

"I guess the greenest patch is right here where we are. We must have caught the sun just right."

"That we did. All of us." Todd indicated the small leaves. "I know just how they felt."

Todd was still marvelling. "You know, that's how spring should come—all at once."

"I'll admit that it does give it an impact."

As the afternoon wore on and the tide came in, a breeze sprang up. First the boys put on their shirts, then by evening their light jackets. It was a beautiful, clear, fire-red sunset with the mountains across the Inlet sticking white ridges into the fading light; but the heat of the morning had passed, never to return with the same intensity all summer.

The boys were doing small, last minute, finishing-up jobs when they realized they were not alone. Suddenly Mr. Vimri was standing near them. The tide was too high for him to drive. Big patches of rocks on the beach between the sites forced one to drive near the lower water. Evidently he had walked up from his site and neither boy had heard or seen him until he was only a few feet away.

Startled, Buff stammered, "Well, he-hello, Mr. Vimri."

Either the man did not acknowledge the greeting, or else the small jerk of his head was meant to take care of the social graces for he said, without preliminaries, "I'll buy your kings Monday—any that you get."

Buff stared at him. "Well, gee, I'm—I'm sorry, Mr. Vimri. I've already told a Mr. Hamilton that we'd sell to him. I'd have been glad to sell to you since none of the can-

neries are open yet, but Mr. Hamilton is doing some smoking and he's already asked and—"

With an impatient wave of his hand, Mr. Vimri went on, "Business is business. You sell to me. I'll pay a dollar more a fish than Hamilton." With that he turned and started away.

Buff was protesting, "I'm sorry, Mr. Vimri, but I've given him my word. But, say, why do you want to *buy* fish? Aren't you selling?"

For the first time, Mr. Vimri looked disconcerted. "Oh, oh, yeh. I'm just—I'm just scouting for a friend of mine. He's the one that wants to buy—"

Todd interjected, "Mr. Yamasaki?"

Mr. Vimri turned penetrating eyes on Todd. "You know him? You know his name?"

"Well, I-I-I, he stopped here once for directions." Was it a crime to know Yamasaki?

"We'll be up Monday for the kings. Be sure to save them." He left.

Exasperated, Buff shouted at his receding back. "No, I'm sorry. Maybe next time." But Mr. Vimri gave no indication of hearing.

Buff looked at Todd. "If he isn't the *strangest* man! Besides, why is he buying fish? If Yamasaki wants fish, why isn't he here?"

The words were tumbling out so forcefully, Todd put his hand up to shield himself. "I don't know. I don't know. I'm sorry I did it. I mean, I'm sorry Vimri did it."

"Well, you should be. I just don't know what to make

of that guy. Besides, I imagine all this fuss may be over one king salmon at the very best."

"One salmon?"

"It's so early and the kings have been declining, as I told you. But we might hit a good pocket. Maybe the state's conservation efforts will pay off. Who knows?"

"Not I," Todd replied. "I know not about salmon. I know not about Vimri. I know not about Yamasaki."

"Dumb, aren't you?"

"It may amaze you, but I get along fairly well in civilization."

As he lay in bed, listening to the sound of the surf, going over the events of the day, Todd thought, "Today was Spring."

Then his thoughts turned to Mr. Vimri and his happy frame of mind vanished. "It's like watching clouds roll in," he decided. "Buff is puzzled but I'm unhappy about it. I don't like that man and the feeling he gives me."

He fell asleep only to dream of dazzling green buds bursting into leaves like a time exposure speeded up; then suddenly dark fog crept in and the tender new leaves were hidden.

VII FISH IN NETS AND FISH STOLEN

Monday morning the boys were up early and they were nervous. "We'll just tackle the inner nets, or the beach nets," Buff said. "We'll not even try the outer ones yet."

They loaded the nets on the back of the jeep, Todd staggering under the weight of the lead ends. "Now, we'll dump each net by each running line and try to have everything all ready by nine o'clock." They drove to the farthest net location. Thoughtfully, Buff looked about. "The tide's still coming in so we can't put these nets very far down the beach. Darn! It will be coming in for two hours yet.

Now, how high will that be?" He paced off some steps. "Do you remember, Todd? How high did it get last time? Let's see, that means we're going to be setting nets on a high, outgoing tide, or maybe right when it turns. Now, let me think—"

Perplexed, Todd could only shake his head. "I don't even see the problem, let alone the answer."

"Okay. We want to get the four nets in the water as quickly as we can, but we can't have them in even one second before nine o'clock. Now the nets are six hundred feet apart. The fastest thing we can do, is to have each net right by the line and ready to go. But we can't leave the nets where the tide will get them . . . Let's do this— we untie the lines where they are fastened to this board or spreader and on this side of the spreader tie the cork line; on this side, we tie the lead line. That keeps the net upright in the water. At the other end, we do the same thing. Get the picture? It's just like it is now except we've sort of inserted a bunched-up net. Then, to get the net in the water, we pull the other end of the running line over there," he pointed about 100 feet away, "and that pulls it through the pulley we set out on the flats. Remember? Remember I told you it's like a triangle? Then, we keep pulling the net until it's stretched in the water. The tide will be high when we set so we'll be fishing right at nine. Then it will go dry in a few hours. We'll probably pick our nets dry on the beach the first time and not have to use the boat."

"Is that good?"

Buff shrugged. "Maybe, for us, because we have so

many things to do. We won't have to worry about getting the boat in the water. But, usually, it's easier to pick from a boat. See, from a boat, you just get one end of the whole net out that way, pulling the boat clear to the end of it. When you pick on dry bank, there are rocks, and the fish are more twisted up, and there is no good way to hold them and get the net off at the same time—they're all dead weight."

Todd looked baffled. "Oh, well," Buff said, "You'll see. Come on, let's dump this first net and go to the next one." He picked what he thought was a good spot, not too near the water, not too far up the beach. Pulling it far by hand was hard on both the net and the fishermen.

The work went slower than they had figured. The nets were heavy, about 120 pounds each. They had to leave the nets high up on the beach and the jeep got stuck in the soft sand. Even Todd began to feel that they might not be doing things just right. It was 8:30 A.M.

"Let's go to the cabin and get a time check. We just can't be off. Not even a minute. We'll grab a cup of chocolate and then go set nets."

They were back at the far location fifteen minutes later. Todd could see that all their neighbors were out. Everyone was running. He sensed the tension in the air. Buff looked as if he were wired. Todd had never seen his cousin like this; but soon the excitement began to mount in Todd too.

"Give me a hand, Todd. Let's get this net pulled right up to the line." They tugged and groaned.

"Three 'til," Buff said shortly. "Now, you understand

what you're to do. Right on the stroke of nine, we untie these knots and tie the net in. As soon as I'm on the last one, you get in the jeep and barrel it to the running line over there. Untie it, wrap it around the trailer, hitch on the jeep, and start driving. That will pull the net out. Keep on the lookout for me and BE SURE TO STOP when I signal you."

"O-O-Okay."

"NINE!"

Todd jumped. "What?"

But Buff was already frantically tugging at ropes. "Nine! Come on!"

It had all sounded so simple when Buff explained it, but it didn't work that easily. In the first place, the knots wouldn't come untied. Todd was still struggling on his first one when Buff was trying to tie the net in. They were in each other's way. "Here, let me get that."

Humiliated, Todd backed up. "Get the lower ones, Todd, the lower ones."

"Oh, sure." He worked with feverish, fumbling fingers to untie those knots. "I got them." As he let go, the buoy on the one end of the line started bobbling down the beach. "Hey, it's going into the water—"

"Well, grab it! We've got to tie the ends of the net to it."

Todd went scrambling down the beach, and into the water. He grabbed the buoy and, gasping, hauled it back up the beach. "Now, let's see: we tie the ends of the net. Where *are* the ends?"

"Oh, good gosh," Buff said. "I know now—we should

have unpiled this net and stretched it out. *Where are those ends?*" He was reaching under the heavy net. "Todd, give me a hand. Let's turn this thing over." They tugged at the net and the ends appeared. "Here, tie yours. Quick."

The boys each secured an end of the net. Todd threw the buoy down and, already the net was being edged and pulled, scooting rocks and pebbles along as it slid toward the water.

"Now, Todd, quick! Get into the jeep and untie the running line, pull it until I tell you to stop, get out and fasten it back to the pole, and pick me up in the jeep." His voice was urgent and Todd was already running. Buff was straightening out the net and trying to keep it from hitting too many rocks and pebbles on the beach. "Tear it to pieces," he said under his breath.

As Todd jumped into the jeep, his heart pounding, he kept saying, "Let it start! Let it start!" It did, beautifully, and he was so engrossed in revving the motor, shifting gears and trying to manipulate the deep, soft sand, that he didn't hear Buff yelling or see him waving his arms frantically.

Aware that Todd was not going to hear him and that he could not catch up with him fast enough, Buff gave up and dashed back to the net. They hadn't noticed when they tied one of the ends, but they had reversed the cork and lead lines so that the net was crossed in the middle. "Oh, no! Oh, no!" he kept saying. He dashed to the top end where the wooden stretcher was. The other end was already in the water. Hastily he untied the knots, dashed to the middle of the net, turned it, spread it out right and ran back to tie the proper ends to the stretcher. He had just tied the second knot, when he felt the pull on the net. He watched it go out until it was tighter, tighter, tighter, enough! He waved at Todd. Todd kept right on going.

Panicky, Buff began running. He waved his arms and shouted. If Todd didn't stop soon, he might pull the whole pole out or snap a rope, or—. Buff ran blindly, his feet and legs heavy in the rubber wading boots which sank into the soft sand. When he got to the jeep, it had stopped and Todd jumped out. "Gosh, Buff, I'm stuck. I can't go any farther."

Panting, exhausted, Buff sank against the jeep. "Thank goodness! Didn't you hear me yell? Didn't you see my wave?"

"No, I was looking at the soft spot in the san— Buff! I'm sorry! I forgot! Did I do any damage?"

Still panting, Buff shook his head. "I don't think so. I guess the ropes and the posts have more power than this jeep and they stopped you. But I wasn't sure. Well, come on, now, go tie that line."

Todd, anxious to make up for his goofing, ran quickly to the front of the jeep. He began unwinding the taut rope, without considering how taut it was. At the last loop, the pressure on it jerked the rope violently. Todd's two front fingers caught between it and the bumper. He yelled with pain and fright.

Buff tore around the jeep to him. He grabbed the rope to take some pressure off. Straining with every ounce of strength he could summon, Buff pulled up on the rope

95

until Todd could free his fingers. When the rope slid on through, the weight was all on Buff. He staggered backwards. "Holy cow!"

Todd grabbed for the rope and managed to snub it around the front of the jeep. "What is making it pull so hard?"

"I don't know. Can you hold it if I go tie it to the post?"

"I think so."

Cautiously Buff dropped his hold, and at a nod from Todd he dashed to the post. There he wrapped the rope and tied it securely.

He ran back to Todd. "Did it hurt your fingers?"

"Well, it didn't do them any good, but I don't think it will bother too much. I mean, you know, just a usual numbness, like your brain on exam day."

But Buff was so preoccupied, he didn't even hear the little joke. "Thank goodness. It could have taken them off. I'll come back and check the net later. Let's get out of here."

"Get out of here?" Todd was momentarily befuddled.

"Yes, yes," Buff said impatiently, already tromping on the accelerator. "Three more nets to get in the water." With a sput of sand, the jeep was off up the beach. "See? It was not really stuck. That was just the net pulling so hard."

Buff talked all the way to the next location, "Now this time, we'll be sure we tie the right ends. I'll try to help 'walk' the net down so it doesn't get tangled. This time, you watch carefully for signs . . ."

Todd nodded. His fingers throbbed. His legs and arms

96

ached. He was sure he hadn't had breakfast or, if he had, it was so long ago it did not count. But underneath the physical aches was a mental anguish. He had made a serious mistake. He had failed Buff. The reverie was short and bumpy for soon the jeep jerked to a stop and Buff leaped out. Todd followed.

"Okay, Todd, let's pull this net into place." They heaved and tugged. "Now, this time, we're going to straighten this thing out. Let's see, this is the lead line and I'll follow it down . . . this is the lead line down here. Okay, tie them. . . . Oh, you haven't got the other untied yet? Here, let me." Todd hopped about, trying to stay one knot ahead of Buff, helping, yet moving out of the way if Buff caught up to him.

"Okay—jeep!"

"Huh?"

"Quick! Take the jeep to the running line."

Todd bolted for the crazy vehicle. Panicky, he realized he couldn't remember where the post was that this running line was tied to . . . oh yes, there it was. After all the work they had put into setting up those lines, how could he have forgotten! "But that," he muttered, "was back in the days of leisure."

He wrapped the line about the jeep and started driving with it. He could feel the net begin to move; the jeep ground down deeper into the sand with the effort. Then he suddenly realized with a shock that again he had forgotten Buff. "Oh, my gosh!" He looked back and saw that Buff was motioning him on and on. He sighed with relief. It was not easy trying to keep an eye on his end of the rope, watch for the soft spots on the beach, keep the jeep running, and never let Buff out of his sight. Then he saw Buff motion, and he jammed on the brakes.

As Buff caught up with him and jumped on the jeep, he said, "That was a little better. Got her all tied up?"

Todd nodded yes. "And no fingers pinched!" he added.

By the time the last net was in the water, Todd was in a daze with his stomach churning. "Boy, the people who complain about the tensions of city life, just don't know what they're talking about!"

But Buff didn't hear him. "Nets in the water!" he shouted gleefully. "Nets in the water!"

There were times, Todd thought dourly, when Buff's mind was a single-track affair.

"Aren't they pretty? Aren't they something?"

For the first time Todd looked out at the nets. He really had not seen that far before: only to the next rope, the next spot of sand, the next dash in the jeep. He looked about. There the spanking white corks in four long, neat lines, danced in the waves. The sun was beginning to shine. The mountains in the distance were white above pink and lavender valleys. Farther up the beach other corks bobbed about. "They look like rows of ducks in a giant shooting gallery," Todd said.

But Buff was looking at them with expansive, proprietary pride. Todd could identify that expression. The last time I saw that look, he told himself, was when Cousin John was showing us his rows of corn back in Illinois.

Buff was climbing into the jeep. "Let's go." He kept his

eyes on the water as he poked along. "You know, Todd, that water had me fooled. It isn't going down so fast. How late is it? Let's see: quarter of twelve." His voice held a wail. "Oh, no! We've *got* to do better than that! Why, all the nets should be out in half an hour, at most. Well, we learned things this morning."

"Is it really so important to get the nets in that fast?"

"Yes, it is. For one thing, we've only got twenty-four hours to fish and every second counts. But the main thing is that quite often, the first few minutes are the best. I don't know why. Guess you catch them unaware. If *you* don't get them, then most likely your neighbor will. So everyone breaks his neck to hit that water and beat everyone else."

While Buff talked about fishing, and what you had to know to be successful, Todd's head drooped. He couldn't remember ever having been so tired in his life. They tumbled out at the cabin, Buff still explaining and talking; Todd half asleep.

"Let's just have crackers and peanut butter and milk now. I think we can pick those nets before the water gets down. Then, after a few hours, we can pick them dry— that is, if there's anything to pick. Okay, Todd?"

"Why, sure. Crackers and peanut butter sandwiches are just what I expected—but, I was hoping I'd be wrong."

Buff was much too excited to notice attempts at humor or any indication of tiredness. "How does he do it?" Todd marvelled. "Does he gobble vitamins all winter and just sit and store it all up for summer?"

Soon they were out again, pushing and shoving the dory. "No use," Buff gasped. "Go get the jeep. We'll give it a shove with that. We've got to get this thing anchored out on some kind of line so we can leave it in the water. It's just too heavy to fool with this way. Something else we learned this morning."

Todd shook his head as he ran for the jeep. Buff was getting to be a real nut on learning things, while he had hoped to put his poor crammed skull on vacation this summer and not let a single thought creep in!

As soon as the dory floated, Buff yelled to Todd. "Okay, I'll get it ready. You take the jeep back to the cabin and bring our rubber pants and jackets and the fish picks."

"Fish picks?"

"Yes. You know, those little iron hook-like things with the red wooden handles. They're hanging there by the door."

"Is that what they are? I thought they must be bent ice picks or something." He backed the jeep up and started on his errands.

On his return, the boys got settled in the boat and Buff started the engine. As it began put-putting, Buff shouted to Todd. "Now, help me remember where those running lines might be. They might be floating now and we might get them caught in the prop. We've got to cross over where they are. Let's see, this one should be about over . . . here . . . there, now we should be across."

Todd was trying to visualize the triangle from the running lines showing on the bank but he saw no way in the

100

world to judge with any accuracy where the lines were now that they were covered with water. Besides he was having other troubles. The Inlet was not particularly bad, for the Inlet, but the dory was slapping into waves and settling into some pretty deep troughs. "Oh, boy," he said. "I'm really and truly glad now that I didn't have anything but crackers and peanut butter."

Buff maneuvered the boat to the end of the first net. "Okay, now, grab onto the net and hang on." He cut the motor.

Todd made a blind stab, leaning over the side of the rocking boat. He grabbed a rope, not at the best place, but he held tight until Buff got there and gave him a hand. "Okay, bring her over the boat."

They pulled the net over the bow of the boat, then Buff crossed over the net to the other side so that the boys were facing each other with the net about in the middle of the boat.

"Now, we just keep pulling ourselves along the net, pick out any fish, and let the net back out over the other side and it's fishing again. Simple?"

It certainly seemed so. In fact, they were going so fast, a button on Todd's sleeve caught in the net, and he almost went over with it. "Hold it! Hold it!"

"Gosh, Todd! I'm sorry. I didn't see that fool button. Tonight we'll take every single thing off our clothes that could possibly catch—buttons, buckles, anything. We'll tie with cord if we have to."

Shaken, Todd still managed a feeble joke. "Never mind,

101

I kind of had the feeling I should be leaning over the side anyway."

"Sick?"

"Not exactly, but I've felt better."

"Just say so. We can stop and rest, or I can take you back to shore. After all, this is mostly practice anyway. We aren't catching anything."

"I think I can manage," Todd said. But the boat was doing some awful sloshing and rocking.

"You know, I've seen these nets so full of fish that you could hardly—"

"Buff! Buff! Help me! There's a fish or something in this net. I can't lift it."

Excitedly, the boys pulled and tugged together. "Holy mackerel! No, that's not right. It's not a mackerel, is it? I mean—careful now. Oh, look! Oh, he's a monster!"

Buff reached over the side of the boat with a gaff hook and grabbed the salmon and together the boys hauled the king aboard. Involuntarily, Todd moved over a bit and had a notion to pick up his feet. The giant thing flounced and floundered. His huge tail came down SPLAT! The boat rocked.

"You mean you put them right in here *with you*?"

Buff could not help laughing. He was high—high with spring, high with fishing, high with a king. "No, we charter a yacht to follow along behind us."

The king was wrapping himself in a wild tangling of the net. Buff looked about and picked up a hammer from the front of the boat. He clouted the king on the head.

102

"There. That will make things easier for all of us." He looked at Todd. "Well, let's take him out. There may be others waiting."

Appalled, Todd looked at the net shrouded brute lying in front of him, still flopping a bit, his mean-looking teeth resting not more than an inch from his toe. "*How?*"

Buff laughed. "Lesson number one in learning to pick fish."

Todd flinched. "There's that word again."

But already Buff was working at the fish. "Let's see: he flopped this way so we'll pull the net over here . . . he wrapped clear around . . . and now we'll slip this one out . . ." He worked as he talked. He used the small pick to slip under the net and pull it down on the fish, or to work out the net strands that were caught in under the gills. Soon, incredibly, the huge fish fell free in the bottom of the boat. Together they exclaimed over him, and Todd examined him carefully for it was the first king salmon he had ever seen.

"How much will it weigh, Buff?"

"I don't know. I'm not very good at guessing weights, but I suppose thirty-five or forty pounds."

Todd whistled.

In a happy frame of mind they finished that net, then the other three, but that first salmon was the only fish. Buff, however, refused to be pessimistic. "They'll come. They'll come. I just know it and, college, here I come."

"How many do you expect to get, Buff? I mean, how many fish make a good year?"

"Oh, kings, I'm not really counting on. Everyone of them is gravy. But the season as a whole—well, maybe nine thousand or so if we're lucky."

"Nine thousand!" Todd whistled. "How long would it take me to pick nine thousand fish?"

They were pulling the dory up on the beach when Todd spotted a terrific splashing. The water roiled, and thrashed. "Hey, Buff! Look."

"Another king! Look at him! Oh, I hope he's caught . . ."

"I guess I do too. In those movies at school, I always felt bad when a salmon was caught after that awful trip; but it does seem different now."

Buff was tearing off. "Come on, Todd. He's in shallow water."

Todd raced down the beach after him. The boys kept right on going and ran clear into the water. "Now, be careful. Don't let him get loose. Remember, there's no boat under us. If he gets out of the net, he's gone."

"What'll I do? What'll I do?"

Buff waded to where the king was still thrashing, but more quietly now. Todd took his cue and followed. The waves were sloshing at them and they were now over their knees in water. Trying to help Buff, Todd leaned down to grab a handful of net and fish. Just then the king gave a powerful leap. Todd jumped back, caught his boot in the net, and went floundering down.

Buff grabbed, putting both arms about the fish as if it were a baby. He glanced back at Todd. "Hey, be careful."

Drenched, spitting and sputtering, Todd said, "Thanks for the warning." He staggered to his feet. One boot was still caught and he had to reach under water to extricate it. His foot slipped on the slick rocks and the waves kept banging at his legs, but finally he was able to help Buff. "What'll we do? Do we want to get him out of the net here?"

"I'm afraid to. He's still alive. Maybe, if we pulled hard enough, we could get this much of the net up on land. Just so we can dump him on the ground. Think we can pull that much on this net? Straighten it out?"

"Well, no, but we can try."

"After all, the tide's going down. I guess I could stand here and hold him until we're on dry ground."

"Why the hurry? Why don't we just leave him?"

"I suppose you're right. But lots of times they slip out. I can't tell how well he's caught. When you catch only one or two kings, you can't afford to lose any."

"How much is it worth?"

"The canneries usually pay around five dollars a fish, but Hamilton said he'll pay me seven and a half for kings under twenty pounds, and ten dollars for anything over. I could get lots more than that, though, if I had time to take it to town and sell it by the pound."

"You mean that's ten dollars you've got hold of there?"

"I imagine." Buff was still holding the king up against his body, net and all. When the fish flounced or a wave hit him, his body bent and rolled, but he managed to remain standing.

105

"You know you look really funny. Listen for that ten dollars you hang on, and I'll see if I can pull this net and give you some slack. You start heading for shore."

They made a few feet, but not enough. "Can't do it, Buff. That old line is getting tight and heavy."

"Okay. Come help me. I think I can get him. I'll give him a crack on the head. Maybe we can horse him in." Todd found a rock and handed it to Buff. After the stunning blow the fish was almost still. Ever so carefully Buff began loosening the net. Todd stood by, ready to grab. Buff unrolled the net, and worked the king loose. He reached in his pocket for his fish pick. "One mesh under the gills and then I think I think he's free. Hang on to his tail."

Todd did as he was told. Suddenly the fish fell free and although Todd held on, he and the salmon went down. "Hold on, Todd, hold on."

Such a slick and slimy thing was that tail. "We're both down here and I've still got him. I think he's dead. But for Pete's sake, get me out of here." He could feel cold, heavy water in his boots, under his shirts, in his pants.

Together, they pulled and shoved the fish ashore. "There! We did it. We've got two." Buff looked at Todd happily. "I don't know about you, but I don't want to carry him up to the fish box. Let's go get the jeep and we'll put them both—Hey! Where'd we leave the other one? Oh yes, he was in the boat, the BOAT! Todd! Did we tie it up when we ran down here?" Frightened, Buff's eyes searched the beach.

"We pulled it up on land, remember?"

Buff sighed with relief. "Yes, but that's not good enough. Thank goodness the tide is going out. If it was coming in, that dory might have floated clear away. We've got to learn to think ahead better!"

"There's that school word. What's with you? I'm going to get the jeep."

The boys put the kings in the fish box. "Todd, you had better go and change your clothes. I want to rig up that hose, if I can, so we can have a steady stream of water running over these fish. That'll keep them cool and clean."

Todd stood there for a moment. "Gee, I never really imagined when I made that old box that these two big guys would be in it. They just about fill it up!"

"They are big, but the box could hold plenty more. Look, Hamilton won't even be around until tomorrow, but, if this were the red run, the fish trucks would drive the beach at every low and every high tide for their pickup."

Todd stood, still staring. "Maybe twenty dollars, huh? You know, this really is fast money!"

"It will get in your blood. But it isn't as rosy as it seems. It takes lots of fish to pay back the investment in equipment and the cost of the site, let alone make a profit."

"Yes, I suppose, but it doesn't look as if you have much invested—a couple of old boats, a couple of old motors, some nets. The cabin is not much. It's probably a lot out here, Buff, but not the way things cost back in Chicago."

"Well, you're right in a way. We're not a General Motors or anything, but if you're talking about a *small* businessman, I imagine we've got about as much in this project as a businessman in Chicago. Of course we're only leasing it on shares but the owner had to buy it. The site itself cost fifteen thousand. Those boats are old, but expensive. The motors could be better, but they cost over eight hundred for the two of them and we had to have some work done on them. Why, Todd, just the rope we used down here cost over a thousand dollars."

Todd's mouth flew open. "A thousand dollars worth of rope! A *thousand dollars—*"

"Yes, a thousand dollars. Their old manila rope was shot so we had to buy all new and we got this new synthetic-type—"

"Synthetic?"

"Oh, come on, now. Didn't you notice that the rope was different? You know, like nylon or plastic."

Todd looked sheepish. "I don't know much about rope, but you're right: it is different. I never even thought about it. There was so much new to me all at once. Synthetic! So in some ways you guys up here are right up to date, aren't you?"

Buff started up the hill to dig out the spring and see if he could rig a hose in it, so the water could flow into the fish box. As Todd went toward the house he saw a vehicle coming. It was the first one to drive the beach on this tide. The driver pulled up.

"Hi, there! You fella's do any good?" A friendly, open, weatherbeaten face smiled out the window at him.

"Well, sir, we got two nice-sized ones. Is that good?"

"Is that right? Yes, I'd say it's good. Hendrickson down by the next bend picked up six right when they set.

Just smack! smack! smack! right down the line. Benson's didn't get any, but then, you know their site never is good early in the year. Up at the point, they had trouble gettin' their nets out and now the tide's goin' out, so they won't get much fishin' in 'til the next tide. Down at the river mouth, Jake picked up three. Heard they're really fishin' over across and, in my opinion, they'll get more over there than we do here. It's early but it always has been good for kings over there. You say you got two? Well, that's real good, Son, real good. Lots of folks got skunked. Let's see, this is Tolson's old site, I believe. Well, I'll remember and get your news to the folks. Got to drive the beach 'most to Ninilchik. So long and—good fishin'."

Todd stood there, dripping wet and waiting to say something friendly, but he waited too long. With a grin and a wide wave of the arm, the man pulled away. The last thing Todd heard him say was, again, "Good fishing."

Buff came hurrying down the hill. "Who was that? What did he say?"

"I don't know who he was but he said that Benson, no, Jake got—well, up at the point, no, the river mouth—I don't know what he said."

Buff showed his impatience. "How did he say everyone was doing up and down the beach?"

"Let's see: for various reasons, various people either got skunked, or got three, or got six." He looked at Buff helplessly.

Buff was evidently hungry for more news. "Well, what about Sundborg's—"

Todd held up a hand and pointed to the disappearing

vehicle. "There goes the roadrunner with the news. He said so much, I can't remember a word of it." Then he burst out laughing. "That's one guy who won't notice that Vimri doesn't answer. No one even has a chance to answer him."

Buff smiled. "See? Like I told you—Alaska fishermen are the—"

"Friendliest and the *wettest* and *coldest* people in the world. I'm going to the cabin."

"Why don't you? I'll work on this hose a bit and maybe you can rustle up something to eat. Then it will be time to pick low tide."

"Pick? We just picked."

"We pick *every* tide—high and low. Of course, it won't be anything much this evening. Just walk along the nets and check them. Probably won't have any, or maybe one; but, in the red or humpy season, you might have to pick steady the whole period."

Todd stared at him. "The whole twenty-four hours?"

Sounding a little smug, Buff said, "Yep. We fish the whole twenty-four hour period."

"I think some people *like* being dogged tired. I've got to get some nourishment." Todd went into the cabin. He was so wet and miserable, he hated the idea even of taking his clothes off. The barer he got, the colder he was. The garments clung to his skin. He was shaking by the time he got dry jeans and a shirt on. Tired as he was, he decided to start the fire to cook some food. When had this day started? Eons ago! He closed his eyes for a second and

110

saw a jumble of fish and nets, ropes and stones, and frothing water.

He found scraps of paper, a few sticks of kindling wood and started the fire. He added coal and the stove took off with a cheerful roar. He went to the grocery shelves. "It will not be stew or peanut butter," he declared to the wall.

He spotted a can of roast beef. "Oh boy," he almost shouted, "roast beef and mashed potatoes. Let's see: where are the potatoes?" He found the box of instant potatoes and read the directions. "I'd have to mix some powdered milk first and then put it all in a pan—no, I'd have all those pans and pitchers to wash. I can't do it." For a moment it all seemed too much trouble and he longed to be back in his mother's kitchen where wonderful meals appeared without strain or fuss. At home he could have real roast beef, not something out of a can, with mashed potatoes and gravy, and a green salad of fresh vegetables. Now he appreciated the fresh greens you could buy at the supermarket at any time of the year. He leaned against the shelf for a second. Then, frowning, he opened the little can of meat, put it in a skillet and heated it. He checked the loaf of bread Buff's father had brought. It was stale but it was better than crackers. He cut a slice and poured the meat over it and sat down to eat.

As he ate, Todd looked out at the beach and water. The tide was going down and part of the nets were already on dry land; only the last few feet were still in the water and fishing. There didn't seem to be any fish on the ground or splashing in the water.

He fixed himself another plate of meat over bread. Finished, he piled the dishes to soak and placed the pan of water on the stove to heat. He put more coal in the stove and turned the draft and damper down so the fire would not get too hot. He hung his wet clothes on nails to dry. Then he looked at what he had done. "If Mom could see me now," he said softly. "She'd never believe it." With enough proof that independence is not easy, Todd collapsed onto his cot. He didn't hear Buff come in and prepare his own meal, nor did he hear him clean up the cabin and wash the dishes. He didn't know Buff, too, had fallen asleep. But he did hear the alarm clock and he struggled awake. The cabin was warm and full of evening shadows.

Buff was already sitting up. "Hi. You looked so comfortable that I decided to follow your example, but I didn't trust myself. I set the alarm."

Todd yawned and burrowed further into his sleeping bag. "Bully for you."

"You want to go help me pick the nets, or do you want to stay here? I don't suppose there are any fish so I really don't need you. It's up to you."

"Are we going to eat anymore tonight?"

"Tell you what: you go out with me and when we come back I'll fry some bacon and eggs and make some hotcakes."

"I'm coming. I'm coming. What's the tide doing?"

"It's coming in now. Actually, we're too late to pick the far end of the nets from dry land but, as I say, it doesn't

112

matter anyway. During the run, that will be a different story."

The boys put on their hip boots and jackets and went outside. The sky held a few late evening streaks of red in the north, but in the south it looked dark and cloudy. "Looks like a fog rolling in, maybe a storm."

Todd pointed to Vimri's site. "Look at that light. What is it?"

A beam of light shone from Vimri's across the water. "I have no idea. It's coming from the hill, or from above his cabin—I know! That must be what he was fixing on his roof the day we went up there. But why? What does he want with a light like that?"

"To see the water?"

Buff laughed. "Well, maybe. Of course, the boats have lights, but I don't suppose he's planning on navigating his cabin—not unless we have another earthquake and tidal wave, that is."

While they watched, the outline of a boat took shape. Almost the second it came into the glare of the light, the light went off.

"Well, gosh! What do you make of that? What kind of boat was it?"

"I couldn't tell, but it looked good-sized. A drift fishing boat, I guess. I hardly expected to see any drifters out this early in the season."

Todd shrugged. "I guess his light was a signal for the guy. I can't understand it: for someone as unfriendly as Vimri, he has lots of callers."

"He sure does. Well, I guess we'd better pick the nets." The boys drove the jeep to the farthest net, got out and walked along all of it that was out of the water. There were no fish. It was getting much darker and cloudier. There was a breeze and, though the air was fresh and fine, it was chilly and Todd zipped his jacket up.

"Tell you what, Buff, this is simple. I can do it. Why don't I finish and you go start that supper."

"It's a deal. I'll listen to bacon sizzling and Radio Moscow."

Todd enjoyed driving the jeep by himself. He dropped Buff off at the cabin and drove to the next site. As he neared the site nearest to Vimri's location, he saw a vehicle parked near their net, and a man. He speeded up. It was Vimri and he was taking a king from the net!

Todd was at an utter loss to know what to do. Was Vimri really stealing their fish? Or was it a custom to help pick your neighbors' nets?

He hurried up to the net, not knowing what he would say, but the words came out, "Did you make a mistake, Mr. Vimri? This is our net."

The man scowled and continued working on the salmon. "I'm buying and I'm in a hurry. I wasn't gonna' cheat ya'."

"You're buying? Well, did you pick our other nets too, while we were down at the other end?"

"I looked at 'em but there wasn't any." He saw Todd glance at his truck. "Yeh, them two in the back is yours. I got 'em out of the fish box. That's three I owe ya' for."

Todd gasped. "Out of our fish box! Mr. Vimri, Buff had

114

them promised. He told you he wouldn't sell to you. I heard him. You can't have those fish!"

Vimri heaved up the king, walked to his truck and threw it in. He brushed past Todd. "Business is business. I'll pay more'n Hamilton for 'em. Settle up tomorrow." He climbed in the truck and drove off, the three kings in the back of his pickup.

Todd stood rooted in the sand. What should he do? He felt anger rising. How important was it? In a way, he guessed, Vimri was right: business was business and if he would pay a higher price—but no! he had heard Buff tell him the fish were already promised to Hamilton. Todd kicked the sand, thinking. What should he do? He walked to the net and straightened it out where Vimri had pulled the king loose. Then he got in the jeep. He would go and tell Buff.

He started the vehicle, then hesitated. The tide was already coming in pretty fast. Soon they wouldn't want to drive the beach, especially at night. Because of the clouds it would get dark early. He was actually closer to Vimri's cabin than theirs. He made up his mind. He would just go up to Vimri's and take his three fish back. He'd just pick them right up and throw them in the jeep. When Vimri saw that he meant business, he wouldn't argue. Mr. Vimri must be told that, perhaps, he could have the fish from the next period, but he couldn't have these, and that was all there was to it.

It all sounded reasonable to Todd as he thought about it, but nearing the cabin his heart began to pound. It was

this feeling he had. He knew it was silly, but Vimri and
that cabin always gave him the creeps. He tried to make
out Vimri's pickup. Maybe he would just take the three
fish and not say anything to him; then, if Vimri missed
them and came up to the cabin tomorrow, he would ex-
plain. "After all," he muttered, "they are our fish."

There were lights in the cabin and in one of the out-
buildings. He prudently shut off the jeep. Sounds didn't
carry at all here on the beach with so much counter noise
from the wind and the surf, but still—. He got out and
walked around the corner of the house. A vehicle was
backed up to the outbuilding. He stepped into the circle
of light and there he beheld one of the strangest sights he
had ever seen and one that would stay with him all his life.

A naked light bulb hung from a swaying extension cord
supported by nails. It cast a small pool of light over the
scene. There stood Vimri, Yamasaki, and a man he had
never seen before. The three king salmon were laid out on
the opened-down tailgate of the truck and Vimri was
butchering one. Yamasaki wrapped a small, blue-black
automatic pistol in plastic and handed it to the third
man, who was nearest the fish. A work table in the room
seemed full of guns, plastic, wooden boxes, and a few
things that didn't register with Todd in that ghastly
moment.

The air was full of tension, irritability, electricity. Vimri
said, crossly, "Let's get a move on! That tide's comin' in."

Yamasaki retorted just as crossly, "Why don't you work
faster? Why didn't you have this done? I'm no fisherman

117

and I'm telling you right now, on any future loads, I'm not goin' to mess around in all this fish slime."

"Ain't you the pretty one? Don't wanna' mess in fish slime! Sure like to mess in guns and money, though, don't you?"

"You said it and that's ALL I contracted to mess around in. You're the lousy fisherman. You have this ready next time."

"I *tried*. Can I help it if there's no fish yet? For a Japanese you don't know much about fishing. You and your time tables."

"Just because I'm a Japanese doesn't mean I need to know anything about fishing. You're the fisherman and you don't seem to know anything about fishing!"

"Is that so?"

Suddenly, the third man spoke up quietly. "For Pete's sake, you guys, knock it off. We're all in this. We all know our timing was off. We have some fish and we're doing the best we can. Now, get those kings cut open and get the guns inside. Here's a box I built: it's got a false bottom. Just toss the kings on top. We'll get a decent load out of this yet. Just don't press our luck. Take it easy. Fishing will pick up. There'll be more. Our contacts will have to wait." The man worked swiftly as he talked, and his words had a calming effect. Vimri and Yamasaki worked faster, too.

Yamasaki was still grumbling under his breath at Vimri, however. "Set up a whole international deal like this and not even know when the fish run starts. Huh."

Todd could not grasp the meaning of it all, but he

118

knew, even if he was from the streets of Chicago, that this was not ordinary Alaskan fishing talk. He also knew that he had better get out of there. He began backing up as quietly as he could and, when it seemed safe, he turned and ran for the jeep. He must get Buff.

VIII A FISHY PLOT IS UNFOLDED

Breathlessly, he related all he could remember to Buff.

"Guns!" Buff echoed.

"You know, little black automatics. They had them right in the fish—stuffing the kings full, covering up boxes full of them with fish on top—"

"Todd, who are *they*?"

"There was Vimri, and Yamasaki, and the other fellow I told you about that I never saw before."

"*Guns*," Buff repeated. "I can't imagine—you must be kidding me."

A Fishy Plot is Unfolded

For once Todd was impatient with his older cousin. "For crying out loud, Buff, I'm not kidding. I didn't imagine it. You know what's the matter with you? You just can't believe anyone up here is a crook. You always think that *you've* done something wrong. I told you from the start that Vimri was weird. Don't you know that bad people can live anywhere? Or do you think they just live in awful places like Chicago?"

Startled, Buff jumped to his feet. "You know, you're right. If someone's an Alaskan or a fisherman or a home-steader—well, I just think they're one of us or something, and that all the bad people live someplace else—doing things you read about in a book. You're right! You've been right all along. I've been the stupid one."

For a moment Todd forgot the chilling spectacle of men and guns and he glowed under these words from Buff.

But Buff was not standing by philosophizing. He was grabbing up his coat. Once he finally made up his mind, action followed. That was the way one lived in Alaska.

"Where are you going?"

"To size up the situation. There's something illegal going on at Vimri's and we've got to find out what it is."

"We must do it?"

"Sure. Who else can? It's almost dark. We'll sneak up there and do some spy work; find out more about those guns you saw—and then go report it to the authorities. The tide's coming in so fast, we can't drive out tonight anyway. And I guess whatever they are doing is going to continue—"

121

"Yep. Sounded that way. That one guy said that fishing would pick up and things would work out yet."

"Okay. Good. So we'll just go find out what we can."

Todd was hesitating at the door.

"Todd, I think it's our duty. Now, I'll tell you: you've done quite a bit. If you'd rather not go, it's okay, this will just be my turn."

"Oh no, I'll go with you. It's just that, well, Buff, it might be dangerous. There *is* a pile of guns up there."

"Oh, maybe so." He considered a moment. "We'll just have to be careful not to be seen. It shouldn't be hard. It's almost dark—as dark as it will get tonight—the tide's coming in which will hide the noise, and they sound busy. They won't be idly looking around." He shrugged. "Besides all those guns probably aren't *loaded*."

With a sigh and a nod of his head that expressed admiration for Buff, and resignation too, Todd followed Buff out of the cabin to the jeep.

"We'll drive about as far as our last net. Then, we'd better get out and walk, and keep under cover as much as we can. The boulders will help."

"Amen," Todd said fervently.

As they skirted from rock to rock, Buff whispered instructions. "We should split up."

"To make it twice as easy to catch us?"

Buff couldn't help a chuckle, but they were both almost grimly serious soon after.

There seemed to be even more frenzied activity around the cabin than before. Dark figures were going back and forth from the shack to a big dory pulled up to the water's edge. As they watched, the light on top of the cabin went on, and swept over the water. There was a hoarse honk from out in the Inlet somewhere. "What do you make of that?" Todd asked.

"Just what we saw before. That light is a signal and so's the horn." As Buff said that, the boat swung into the light and, when it did, the light suddenly shifted and went straight up into the air.

"What do you make of *that*?"

"Well, as long as it doesn't cost anything to guess, it may be they want the boat to see the light, but no one else to see the boat."

"Sounds reasonable, but why?"

"I think I'm beginning to understand, but let's find out more first."

"Tell me what to look for. I don't care if you guess wrong. I'll never tell."

"I can't guess it all, but it must be that this boat has come to get those guns all covered up with fish. But after that, I give up. Of all the crazy things—loading and un-loading, and hiding, in *fish* of all things. Where do you suppose they are taking them? And why?"

"Oh no. I'm not on the answer end. I'm on the question end." Todd thought a moment. "But, wait a minute, Buff, I know something. When I was here before, Vimri and Yamasaki were arguing and Yamasaki said something like . . . 'an international deal like this and you don't even know when the fish run starts.' "

Buff turned and looked at his cousin in the dim light. His tone was hushed and he gave an ominous sound to the word in the night, "*International?*"

"I just know that's what he said."

"Wow! I mean, *wow!* This may be more than we bargained for. Listen, Todd, I'll tell you. I want to sneak down by that dory they're loading and see if I can find any clues there. There seem to be only the three guys. I'll wait until I think I can make it, and then crawl over there. You know what the setup is out back so you sneak around there again. Okay?"

Todd didn't much like the idea of separating or of being where all those guns and grim-faced men were, but he hesitated only a second. "Okay."

Buff gave him a pat on the shoulder. "Now, DON'T GET CAUGHT."

Todd gulped. "That would be nice."

The boys parted company and Todd sidled around the edge of the cabin to where he had seen the packing activity earlier. He knew what to expect and he knew how to be careful, but his luck had run out. He had the misfortune to peek around the corner of the house at the exact second that Yamasaki happened to glance in that direction. Todd's heart sank. He ducked back into the shadows, but the damage was done.

The Japanese yelled, "Quick! It's that kid!" Todd considered a split second. Should he run toward Buff? Should he yell? No, Buff might not hear him, but the other men would. He made a dive toward the hill behind the cabin. Perhaps he could lose Yamasaki in the brush. He only had another running jump or two to the cover of the alders when the blow fell on the back of his head. Lights exploded in his head and that was the last he remembered as he crumpled down in the soft sand. There was a hurried consultation over him between Vimri and Yamasaki.

"Do you think the other kid's around?"

"I dunno'. This is the one I talked to this evening. He probably came back to get his kings. Well, anyway, take care of him."

"Whaddya' mean, take care of him?"

"I mean take care of him. He's got to have an accident."

"Then, *you* give him the accident. I'm not a fish butcherer and I'm not a kid murderer. I had a nice clean deal set up and you fouled it up all along the way. If you had handled these kids right, we wouldn't have had this trouble."

"All right, all right. I'll take care of him. I'm not a kid murderer either. I'm just going to help him have an accident. Now get out there and finish up. I'll be right there. We've got to get that dory out to the *Sue X* and get her loaded." He turned, dashed into the storage shack for some supplies, then picked up Todd, threw him over his shoulder and started walking a few yards up the beach.

Buff, in the meantime, had managed to get to the water's edge where the dory was floating. He was just about to take a peek over the top when he heard someone coming. His heart pounding, he waded into the surf and around the back of the dory to hide. With the cold waves pounding his back, he still managed to remain upright by leaning now and then on the side of the dory,

125

while the man, on the other side, threw in a box. Stumbling, cursing, and breathing heavily, he stacked the case in the boat, then turned and went back up the beach. Buff edged to the shore side of the boat where the water wasn't so deep, but it was too dark and the sides of the dory were too high for him to see inside. He pulled himself over the side and jumped into the boat. The usual coils of rope and miscellaneous gear lay about, things one could find in almost any dory, plus several wooden boxes. There were big plastic bags in a pile and a canvas tarp covering one stack of boxes. He had just pulled back the tarp to investigate when he heard voices. He crouched down. Then the voices were near enough so he could make out the words.

"All right. Everyone pile in. We've got to get out to the *Sue X*."

Buff cast about wildly for an avenue of escape. They were getting into the boat to leave! Wisely, or unwisely, he edged behind the stack of cases and pushed himself into the very tip under the bow of the dory. He pulled some of the tarp about him. One man was already boarding!

"Hold 'er steady a minute, Yamasaki."

"Okay. You in? Shall I untie it?"

"Not 'til Vimri gets here. Where *is* he?

"He'll be along in a second. We found a kid looking around the corner of the building. Vimri's going to help him have an accident."

"A kid? An accident? What a mess this has turned out to be."

"I agree, but it'll be okay, I think. We'll get the bugs all ironed out and have those guns flowing to Japan just as regular as a high tide on the beach. Don't worry about that kid. Vimri will make it look good."

Buff heard all these things and a chill spread from around his heart clear down to his toes. What was happening this very minute to Todd? What should he do? Should he try to stay hidden? He couldn't possibly overcome two men and get out of the dory. . . . Maybe if he took them by surprise? He tried to watch from behind the tarp. It would take a few seconds for him to crawl out around the boxes—then if he could knock one of them off his feet —maybe he could jump out of the dory? But no, the other man would be on him, and Vimri was still on shore. Should he try to sneak off the boat? Throw something in the water in the other direction, as people did in the movies, and when the men looked that way, crawl out and slip over the side. True, he would make a big splash, but they might think it was a king splashing. Even as Buff was considering a method of escape, it was too late: Vimri was untying the line and wading out to the dory.

"Let's get this dory underway." As Vimri heaved his body over the side, one of the men started the motor and the dory pulled away from the shore. With the noise of the engine, the only thing Buff could hear the man say was . . . "all taken care of . . ."

A terrible grief and dismay filled Buff. What had he let happen to Todd? He was older, he should have known better. But what he should have done was of no help now. He had to think. He had to get out and he had to find Todd. If Todd had to have an "accident" well, maybe, just maybe, it hadn't happened yet—whatever it was.

As the dory pulled alongside the bigger boat there were general greetings, brief and subdued. "Where you guys been? Come on, let's get this load on. I got to make real tracks while it's still dark. This may be a good plan and it may be safe, but I'll feel better when I'm in international waters." The men lifted and groaned and unloaded the boxes. One man on the *Sue X* seemed to do a lot of talking, mostly to Yamasaki. Buff figured he was the skipper.

Buff was huddling farther and farther back into his corner as the pile of boxes began going down. Would they pull the bunched-up tarp to check behind it? True, it was almost dark—but not dark enough to hide a six-footer. He had better be ready. But what could he do?

Then he got the break he had been hoping for. Yamasaki, still talking to the skipper, climbed on board the *Sue X* and told the third man of his party, "Come on, Alec, and give us a hand up here. Vimri can get the rest of those boxes."

Buff held his breath. This had to be it. This was the last chance! Vimri was now the only man on the dory and, just as he reached within inches of Buff to pick up a box, Buff swung up with all his might. Startled, Vimri fell backward, yelled, and dropped the box. Buff then shoved Vimri, using all his strength. The man teetered for a moment, then went over the side. His yells and splashing brought the other men swiftly to the scene.

Voices shouted: "Man overboard!" . . . "Someone's on

that dory!" . . . "Get down there!" . . . "Hey, what's going on?" . . . "Hey!"

But the few seconds of confusion were all Buff needed. In three long jumps he was at the stern of the dory. He fumbled just a second with the outboard, then it caught, and he threw it into gear. The dory veered away from the *Sue X* and left pandemonium. Vimri was yelling for help and everyone on board the *Sue X* was yelling back. But even as the dory streaked away, Buff heard the splash of the skiff being lowered. He knew he didn't have much time, and he didn't even know where to look for Todd. He headed the dory straight for shore. As the bow hit the beach with a smack, Buff was over the side and running up the bank yelling, "Todd! Todd!"

The first sensation Todd had of returning consciousness was a terrible pain in his head. Then he felt a wrenching, bone-shattering cold, and wetness. Where was he? As he tentatively put out a hand, his benumbed brain was sending frantic signals of distress. He half sat up. He was on the beach. It was almost totally dark now. He couldn't see a thing, but HE WAS IN THE WATER! The tide! The tide was coming in! He was in the way of the tide. He was lying on his back and was in almost an inch of water up at his head. His legs were already covered. With a start, he jerked upright, started to get up, but discovered he couldn't. A moan escaped. His leg! What was wrong? Gingerly, he felt down the length of the leg. It wouldn't move. "Why, I'm anchored!" he said aloud.

Then flashes of memory came back. The scene at

Vimri's: the fish, the boxes, the guns, the sprint toward the alders, and then oblivion. Why, they had put a weight on him and left him to be covered by the tide. "I suppose they will come back when the tide starts to go down and cut this thing loose so it will look like another accident. 'Fell and hit his head and then drowned,' would be the verdict. Buff said someone gets killed every year in this fishing game. . . ." His brain began to focus. "Buff! Where do you suppose Buff is? Is he—is he out here too? Is he about to get covered by the tide?" He was talking aloud and his teeth were shaking and chattering with cold and fear.

"I've got to get free. Buff may be worse off." Frantically, he began pulling and straining at the weight. He reached down. How was the weight fastened? There was a rope. Was it just tied? The water was creeping and sloshing in, faster, deeper, and colder. Was he tied to a rock on the beach or on a weight? He just couldn't tell. He tried to reach far enough forward to feel the rope, but his head was splitting and his leg was under water. Cold, shaking, and sick, he reached in his pocket and found his knife. Carefully, ever so carefully, he leaned forward and began cutting at the rope. HE MUST NOT DROP THAT KNIFE! He was gritting his teeth from pain and exhaustion. He felt the rope give. He jerked at his leg. No, not yet. The water, now that he was sitting up, was already over his lap. Nearly blind with pain, and stiff with cold, he carefully ran his hand over his foot. There was a wire. It felt like a piece of baling wire wrapped about his foot. He began unwinding it. When he pulled it free, he could move his foot. He quickly flipped over on to his hands and knees to try to crawl higher up on the beach. Where was he? Where was the jeep? Where was Buff? If only he could make it to the jeep! But it was so dark and he was so sick. Just then, he heard a call, "Todd! Todd!"

Oh, what a welcome sound. "Buff! Buff! Help me! Quick!" Soon there were strong, helping hands supporting him, getting him up on his feet.

"Todd! Oh, Todd, am I glad to see you. Are you okay?" Buff was so full of relief, he didn't know whether he was laughing or crying.

Todd struggled to keep from slipping into unconsciousness again. "I'm okay, I guess. Are you? Where's the jeep? I can't walk."

"It's not far. Come on, lean on my shoulder. They're after us, or at least they will be as soon as they pull Vimri out of the water."

"What do you mean?"

Buff was struggling with Todd, half pulling and half pushing him toward the jeep. "Oh, I took a boat ride by mistake with them and I had to shove Vimri overboard to get away. But they had a skiff on the *Sue X* and I imagine they'll be after us soon, unless they have to take off in a hurry. Maybe they'll think no one will believe us anyway —just a couple of kids."

As they got to the jeep, Buff practically picked Todd up and rolled him into the seat. "After what they did to me, I don't think we should count on their just forgetting us," Todd managed to say.

131

"What did they do to you?"

"I'm not sure. I got a conk on the head and when I woke up, I was all tied up and the water was coming over me."

Buff climbed into the jeep next to Todd. "No, I don't think they're going to forget about us either. . . . Listen!"

Even as he spoke, they heard the sound of the outboard nearing the beach. Buff quickly turned on the ignition. "Just let this fool jeep start," he said under his breath. The engine caught, sputtered, then caught again. Buff breathed a sigh of relief. "Whew," he patted over on the seat where Todd was. "Hang on."

As they labored up the beach, close to the cliff in order to skirt the rising tide, Buff peered anxiously ahead, over the frame of the non-existent windshield. He must try to dodge the rocks and boulders. "Todd, can you think yet? How bad do you feel? What shall we do? I don't know how far we can drive with this tide. It will go over 19 feet tonight and I just know we can't get very far."

"I don't know, Buff. I feel awful. I'm terribly cold and sick, but I'm alive. I want to stay that way. So let's walk the beach. Let's climb the hill. Let's do anything, but LET'S GET OUT OF HERE!"

They were nearing their shack. Buff pulled up and let the jeep idle for just a second. Should they go in and get Todd dry and try to hide or hold them off? There were no guns or weapons of any kind in the cabin. Would the men pursue them clear up here, or would they be satisfied to have run them off? Buff was afraid he knew the answer.

With a sudden decision, he shifted into gear and pulled

away from their cabin. He struggled out of his jacket and threw it over Todd. "Here. Try to cover up a little. I'm afraid you're too cold and sick for this ride but I dare not stop to fix you up. If it's okay with you, we'll drive as far as we can. If we have to, we'll pull the jeep up on the hill any place, and walk the rest of the way."

Todd lay there, shivering. He pulled Buff's jacket around him. He roused a bit and said, "Do you know now what it's all about, Buff?"

"I got a lot of answers. Maybe not all of them." He looked over at Todd. "Still awake?" Todd's head was lying limply along the back of the seat.

"Yes, and I can hear you. What's it all about?" He wanted to know but the words came out slowly and with an effort.

"Well, for one thing, they are hiding guns in the fish and taking them on board a fishing boat and the fishing boat is headed for international waters. I don't know why—maybe to sell them to someone else out there. Probably the fish are just a trick to make the boat and all look legal. From what they said, it sounds as if the guns are headed for Japan."

"Japan? That's a long way off. Does that make sense?"

Suddenly, Buff spoke with confidence. "Yes! Yes, it does. Now, I betcha' I know. In Japan all firearms have to be registered and this has made a big black market in guns. I read about it in the paper not more than a month or so ago. A lot of guns are being slipped into Japan from this country and they haven't been able to find out how it's being done. Oh, they caught one or two guys, but they know there are more." Buff was talking a mile a minute. "I don't know where the guns are coming from—" he broke off. "Boy, oh boy, Todd, we may really be on to something!"

Holding his head in his hands, Todd moaned, "May be on to something! I haven't doubted that for most of the time I've been here and, after this evening, I *know* we are."

"What I mean is, well, this is more than I . . . we're going to have to get out of here and get word to the police!"

Todd moaned again. "I liked that first part, anyway. Getting out of here is all I can think about."

Buff was again going over all the facts they had discovered, trying to pin them together, but Todd could only lie there, his head throbbing.

It was a wild, desperate ride. Buff was afraid to use the headlights and so he had to keep peering into the darkness to try to avoid deep water, the rocks, the boulders. Once Todd roused and asked, "Are they chasing us yet?"

"I don't think so. At least they aren't using any lights if they are. Maybe they are still looking for us somewhere near their cabin. Try to relax. We'll be at Sundborg's soon."

But just as he said that, strong headlights flashed on, down the beach, and began moving toward them.

"Oh oh. Oh oh." Buff pressed down on the gas.

They were nearly there when the water caught up with them. Buff looked at it with dismay. "I've got to head into

this rock pile or give up. Hang on, Todd, I'll be as easy as I can." Laboriously, the jeep crawled over the rocks, one wheel precariously climbing up on a boulder, then slamming down. There was a sickening scrape and bang. "Oh, no, I think we're high-centered." Desperately Buff shifted into reverse, then slammed it into low. The jeep just sat and spun helplessly.

Buff was about to get out to look the situation over, when his heart lurched up into his throat. There, close, oh so close, was the truck with lights stabbing the darkness. "Quick! They're coming and we're stuck. Todd, get out! We'll have to run!"

Staggering, half running, half falling, the boys hurried over the soft sand, Todd leaning for support on Buff. Although the surf and the rising wind made the usual noise, Buff, alert to all sounds, heard the truck bounce on the rock pile. Then there was silence. He heard a door slam. Yamasaki or someone must be after them, running on the beach also!

He spurted forward and urged Todd on. He glanced back and, sure enough, there was a dark, rapid movement on the beach. A form was running along the side of the headlights' beam. "I'll bet he's making better time than we are. COME ON!" For just a moment he debated. Should he hide Todd behind a boulder? It would be easy in the dark. But no—there just ahead, Sundborg's shack rose darkly on the beach. Apparently they were all in bed but Buff was sure they had been fishing today. "Let them be there," he gasped under his breath.

A Fishy Plot is Unfolded

Suddenly a dog started barking. It was the loveliest sound the boys had ever heard. For the first time in this night of horror, they heard a good sound. It meant people and help and civilization. As the boys pounded up to the shack, Buff shouted, "Mr. Sundborg, Mr. Sundborg, MR. SUNDBORG!" They stumbled up the steps, and a light came on. Still supporting Todd at the door, Buff glanced behind them, up the beach. Their pursuer was very close, but he was not moving. Buff held his breath. Then the door opened.

"Mr. Sundborg! It's me, Buff Sanderson, have you got a gun?"

Just as Buff said that, Todd slipped and literally fell through the doorway. Mr. Sundborg made a grab for him. "Well, whaddya' know? Well, for Pete's sake, what's goin' on?"

"Have you got a gun? They are trying to kill us. They followed us here. *Have you got a gun?*"

"Yeh, yeh. I got a .22 that might keep 'em off. Say, who are we keeping off?" As Mr. Sundborg talked, he eased Todd over onto a bunk. Two other figures were rolling out of sleeping bags. "Come on, boys," Mr. Sundborg said in the direction of the bunks. "Looks like we got trouble."

Swiftly, Buff told them all he knew.

One of the boys asked, "Are you sure he's out there now? Know who it is?"

"No, but the truck was after us right up on the beach. Guess they got stuck on the rock pile too. Then I just saw a man following us nearly up to your cabin. Yamasaki, maybe. Or Vimri. There might be more but I just saw one."

The Sundborgs expressed their astonishment. One of them peeked out from behind the curtain of a window. "Can't see a thing," he reported.

"I don't imagine they'll bother us now that we're in here, but just in case, you'd better have your gun ready."

Mr. Sundborg was shaking his head. "Well, whaddya' know?"

There was a consultation and finally it was all settled. "All right, Ben and Joe, you stay here with Todd. Keep the door bolted and keep your gun ready. Turn out the lights, maybe. Buff and I will walk up to Darlington's. They got a sending set and we'll radio for help."

It was all decided and, as preparations were made, Mr. Sundborg repeated, "Well, whaddya' know? And it started out such a nice dull day for the first day of fishing."

In his relief at escaping thus far, Buff didn't know whether to laugh or cry. As they were ready to leave, he urged them to be careful. "He may be right outside. There are two of us, but if he's got a gun—"

Ben Sundborg turned out the cabin lights as his father and Buff crept out. There was no sound. The dog was quiet. "No sign," said Mr. Sundborg, "but let's spread out a little. If he does spot one of us, it's so dark, the other one could get through."

They had just circled the shack when a dark form stepped from behind Sundborg's fish truck. The hand was raised when Mr. Sundborg lunged. A gun went off. For a split second, Buff hesitated. But the shot had been heard in the cabin and the Sundborg boys were coming. Buff made up his mind. As fast as he could he put one foot in front of the other and sprinted up the beach. It was too far to run all the way, "But I'll bet I set a record anyway," he said aloud. As he pounded on the Darlington door, he thought wryly that he had just done the same thing down the line at Sundborg's. "Just like Paul Revere," he told the dark night.

The door opened. Without preliminaries Buff began, "There's terrible trouble on the beach. Can we radio a message out for help?"

Nothing else has such an effect on Alaskans as a call for help. In a huge, lonely, forbidding country where people are pitted against awesome elements, they are ever alert to such a call, knowing full well that, next time, it may be they who are in need, their own lives that are at stake.

Mr. Darlington rushed to the radio set. "I'm your man. Start talkin'."

It was hours later and Todd was lying in his own cot back at their cabin. His head was propped up on a pillow. He dimly remembered being moved from Sundborg's and a doctor bandaging his head and foot. He looked around the room. Buff was cooking. "Hi. Did I have a knockout drop or something? Or was I still sleeping off the plain old knockout?"

Buff turned and grinned at him. "Hi! How are you feeling? No, the doctor gave you a sleeping pill. Said you'd be dopey. I told him you always are."

Todd raised up on one elbow. "Boy! And I only had

one crack on the head. How do they manage on television when they keep getting conked time and time again?" He sat up. "Well, what happened? Did we find out what it was all about?"

"Sure did. Sorry you missed some of the excitement. We had a doctor down here and some Fish and Game guys, and a patrolman, and, oh yes, the Coast Guard even got in on it."

"Well, what's the story?"

"Just about what we had figured out."

"Tell me again."

"They were smuggling guns to Japan all right, cashing in on the big black market."

"It really wasn't an accident that Yamasaki was Japanese, was it?"

Buff nodded. "Right. He arranged the deal. You saw how they did it. Stuffing the guns in fish and covering boxes of automatics with fish. This boat that we saw out there, the *Sue X,* was bound for international waters to meet another Japanese fishing boat, but the Coast Guard grabbed the boat and the whole crew. The big trouble with their plan this week was that their time table was off. They were in too big a hurry. They needed fish."

Todd rubbed his head. "I'll say they did." He thought a minute. "How about Mr. Sundborg? Was he hurt?"

Buff shook his head. "No, the shot went up in the air while they were wrestling around. Ben and Joe ran out to help their dad." Buff shook his head sadly. "Imagine! Vimri—an Alaskan fisherman trying to shoot his neighbor."

140

"So it was Vimri after us. What a friendly Alaskan fisherman—" Then Todd stopped in the middle of the thought. "Buff! The nets! It's evening again. The period must be over. Did you get the nets in?"

"*We* didn't, but they're in. Got another king too. Todd, you should have seen it. The patrolman and two Fish & Game fellows and Ben and Joe Sundborg were all out there pulling nets for us. Imagine! The Fish & Game people doing that!" Buff doubled over laughing.

For the life of him, Todd didn't see what was so funny about it. "What's the joke?"

"Oh, nothing really, I guess. It's just that people think of them as always making arrests, and that you want to stay clear of them, and here they were throwing rocks out of the nets like everything. The tide had washed a pile of rocks over this end of three of the nets—must have buried them—and you should have seen those fellows throw rocks! I'm glad they helped out. It was real nice of them, but just the same, I'll bet they learned that it isn't always as easy to get those nets out right on the second as they thought it was." He began to laugh again, but Todd didn't see that it was THAT funny. "Besides," Buff said, "it will look good for them in the paper."

"What will?"

"Oh, their pictures. The Anchorage paper sent a fellow down with the Coast Guard. Took pictures of all of it. I forget to tell you. We're heroes! You're even going to get your picture in the paper—bandages and all. You see, we broke up this smuggling ring that they've been trying to

141

get their hands on for over two years now—well, we at least broke up part of it."

"We did?"

"Yep. We're real heroes. How does it feel?"

"Well, mostly, it's a headache."

Buff grinned. "Just wait until your picture is splashed all over the papers, you won't think so then."

Todd looked pleased. "Picture in the paper? Gee! Smuggling ring!" That had a nice sound. "Smuggling ring." He thought a moment how that would sound back in Chicago? They might not know what he meant, or how important it was, when he told how they had caught a dozen kings; or fouled up a running line; or that the humps would run after the reds; but a smuggling ring! That meant something everywhere. He dwelt on the delights and possibilities of telling his family all the details.

"Buff! Buff! What a theme I'll have for next fall when we all have to write, 'What I Did on My Summer Vacation.' Gee, I hope it all comes out in the paper. If I don't have some proof, I'll get a failing mark for being such a liar."

"They said it would be in the papers."

Todd shrugged. "Oh well, I'd rather be an Alaskan fisherman than a hero any day."

Buff's reaction to this was to grin broadly. "Good! You really like it, huh? But, we haven't done much fishing yet, Todd. You'll like it even more later on. It's all been work so far and not much sport. But you wait! It'll get in your blood."

"Yes, I know—and in addition, everyone knows that Alaskan fishermen are the *friendliest*—" His eyes were shining and he was grinning as he ducked one of Buff's boots that sailed across the room at him.